Once In A Glass Wing

No part of this publication may be reproduced, distributed, or transmitted in any form or by any means, including photocopying, recording, or other electronic or mechanical methods, without the prior written permission of the publisher, except in the case of brief quotations embodied in critical reviews and certain other noncommercial uses permitted by copyright law.

The story, all names, characters, and incidents portrayed in this production are fictitious. No identification with actual persons (living or deceased), places, buildings, and products is intended or should be inferred.

Originally published on May 18th, 2022

Once In A Glass Wing

3

The Mardi Town Series

Zineb Bizriken

To the ones who are stuck in a world of books

Chapter 1

In the basket of my bicycle, a single book and a bottle of strawberry milk. Butting my head with the wind, I pedalled straight ahead. The sun and I had risen at the same time today. And so I felt the birds were greeting me along with their sharp noises, on the verge of being annoying. Note that I said on the verge; the line hadn't been crossed yet, though at this rate, it won't take long. My humming of a song that's been stuck in my mind was my counter greeting. Any more and I'll be known as the crazy girl of Mardi Town—another version of the pigeon lady. If I were to go crazy and communicate with birds, I'd rather they compare me with snow white, but that's unlikely to happen. Meanwhile, my eyes were stuck on something other than the road I should have my eyes on. I looked at my book in the basket. It lured me in. I was nearing the library, regardless; it called for me ahead of time. If I could, I'd read while biking; for my safety and other's, I'd keep my eyes on the road. The quiet road, yet to be filled with cars avoiding the morning traffic, not knowing they were already part of it. Opening my necklace, I took hold of the key attached to it to open the back door of the Glass Wing library. This key was always on my neck, not for the reason I lose things with ease, but for the reason, I rarely had pockets in spring or summer clothes. For example, on this day, I wore a long summer dress; no pockets here. And the basket of my bike is out of the question since it'll automatically slip through one of the empty spaces between the bars. Stepping in, I am welcomed by another creature, one slightly bigger than the birds that had flown over my head. A black kitten I'd named Nabi came rushing to my feet with her little paws. She is one of the reasons I clock in so early. Though I wouldn't really call it clocking in; what I do here in the morning is nowhere near work. My entire day in the library doesn't feel like work. First, I pet little Nabi until she's sick of it and tries to bite my fingers—cats are fickle.

Afterwards, I fill her bowls with water and dry food—that brings me back in her favour. Onto my personal routine; our library has a humble sized kitchen—far away from any book—it came with a fridge and a microwave. Employees had an assigned basket and kept their lunch, or perhaps snacks and beverages, in them. I thought it wasn't enough seeing that I practically lived here. I kept ingredients in the fridge and others were gracious enough to yield an entire section of the fridge to me. Using my paycheck, I'd filled the kitchen with additional appliances such as a toaster, a mini oven, a waffle machine, a blender, and a portable stove; all that to make use of those ingredients and have a full on breakfast here, occasionally a dinner as well, it depends on how late I stay. This morning, I wasn't in my best shape and decided on something not-so grand, a toast with strawberry cream cheese to go with my homemade strawberry milk. If you hadn't noticed by now, strawberry is my lover aka my favourite fruit. Behind the library was a garden, and that's where I eat my breakfast, if the weather allows it. I sat at the round and white ceramic table, a book in my hand and a toast in the other. Coming earlier allowed me to have leisure of my time. I got lost in the author's imagination that had merged with mine. Not one sense was neglected. My vision was a vast amount of delicious words. My ears enjoyed the sounds of nature. The scent of fresh grass was as pleasant as an expensive perfume. The taste of strawberries reached my heart, going up a magical path. Lastly, the wind left kisses on the nape of my neck, satisfying the touch. Mornings such as these are a reason to wake up earlier. Finding joy in the little things is the way I live.

I had chosen to re-read one of my favourite novels. It's a classic, the tale of the boy Peter Pan whose horrible personality was only shown to the people who read the book. The movie adaptations had for audience children and thus had to omit some details such as the fact Peter Pan was merciless as he stole those children, only to replace them without a second thought when they'd either grown up or come to resemble him. Nonetheless, it's an enjoyable book. It brings me to adventures on the make believe island and I ask for nothing more. The world I crafted is vaster and more colourful than they could imagine. I'm talking of all the ones that questioned my career choice. I am a young librarian in her early twenties. They think I'll get sick of working in what they call a stuffy environment. They question it, not understanding how happiness differs for each individual. Sorry to disappoint you, but I am but a mere individual as they are. When I was younger, I viewed myself as Wendy from the book I read now, Peter Pan. But I would have made a different choice. I'd wanted to stay in Neverland. Now that I am stable and satisfied with life, things are different. I see no use in leaving this portal who brings me places farther than the Neverland. With the books of this library, I can travel the world and different universes in my seat. Lifting my wrist, I saw the time on my fabric watch. The hour told me to hurry with that toast and milk since work awaited me. Another reason I came early was to fulfil my duties at my own pace; I am a bit of a slowpoke. When I get back in, the first thing I had to do was prepare the reservations. Few books that readers selected online were already in Glass Wing while others would come through the delivery man, Mr. Emoh. These certain books come from other public libraries. As if the book I had to put down wasn't enough of a distraction, Nabi rubbed her body against my legs as soon as I stepped foot back inside. She showed rare signs of affection and it plunged me into a dilemma.

"How nice," I told her, not knowing whether my smile was genuine or counterfeit.

It pained me to leave her, but work waits for none. Instead, I made an agreement with her. It claims that she'll have a piece of my time in due time after I complete my tasks and spend a part of my break time reading. Talking to a cat, I acknowledged that only I could understand the agreement. Nabi will just have to be patient—quite the hard task for a kitten. I let her follow me in my quests and occasionally pet her when organising books on a lower shelf. Luckily for her, many books were to be placed on lower shelves today.

***

"Being here so early is making me look lazy, Salem. The old single lady is the one who should be here all day," Ms. Elgnis said, hanging her black satchel bag on the coat hanger.

11

She fixed her caramel brown curls with a reflection on the window as the wind had ruffled them a bit.

"Don't worry, I'll tell them it's you who fed the cat and turned on the lights," I laughed with her as I continued my work.

These kinds of jokes were our favourite method of communication. We greet each other with humour, hiding the slight bit of truth inside. Ms Elgnis—another librarian—has known me for long. Before they officially hired me, I'd still practically lived here. After school, the first place I went to wasn't my house but here. On weekends, I was here from opening time to closing. She watched over me as I devoured novel after novel. She saw me grow and for me, she's more than a co-worker.

"How's your morning so far?" she asked.

"As it was yesterday."

"Good, then?"

"More than good," I answered, joy seeping from the corners of my lips.

She gave me a nod before going to her station, where she'd do computer work. Ms. Elgnis sang a merry tune on the way. It was a quirk of hers. We were alike on how much we took pleasure in working as librarians, though at first, it wasn't her occupation of choice. In the matter of days and weeks, she came to love it. The power of stories and the effect they have on people had brought on a positive light changing her mind. Working in such an environment, I could meet Ms. Elgnis and talk with people who loved reading just as much as I did. Isn't that happiness? Reading, imagining and forming an opinion is one thing, but to discuss it with other gives you a new perspective. Sometimes, it's the closest you can get to the sequel of a standalone novel. With excitement rising in me to start this new day, I am ready to open the doors and turn on the LED sign. Of course, this library is no boutique on sales day; there is no line forming outside waiting to barge in and get the best deal. No customer comes this early for the exception of my younger self. I have yet to find a rival in this domain. Most people came in the afternoon after their classes or work. We never were as busy as clothing boutiques. Still, my heart beats for this moment. The most interesting people make their way here in the morning. The ones with a peculiar job or a story of their own. At times, authentic stories told by people can be just as entertaining. There are great story tellers out there. I almost fly over to my station hoping these interesting people will come today. For the check-out process, people rely on us librarians and not self-checking-out machines. In Glass Wing we value interactions. Besides, many of our visitors wouldn't be able to use them—children and elderly. Our previous director had decided to never install such machines here. He often said the world was too focused on the future that it failed to realize the present was perfectly fine. Wrong things of the past remained while already good things advanced too fast without a breath in between. Solving should be a priority rather than enhancing. I wholly agreed with him, and that is why I fought with the current director to respect his wishes.

As I waited for someone to place their books on my desk, I sneakily slid a book of mine under to read. I lifted my eyes as often as I possibly could. No rule in our guidebook stated that a librarian couldn't read during work hours, but it was frowned upon. It was an unspoken rule, you could say. I was never scolded for it, but the surprise visits of the director made me nervous. Her presence is quite the treat.

The morning was slow; it was only nine in the morning. At this time, some were on their way or getting ready while some were still asleep, perhaps dreaming of a moon that shined solely for them. Lifting my eyes, I, at last saw the glass doors opening. It was a man who, at first glance, looked like any other. On a closer look, he looked familiar. That is when I realized he had the face of someone that only I in this library could recognize. The lemon tone of his hair, the eyes of a deer and that button nose. Without a doubt, this was Cove, the one I'd last saw as a boy graduating in the same class as me. It was my first time seeing him a man. Cove Evaw's his name. Don't ask me why I remember his last name. He everyone's favourite, starting from the teachers to the students. That's not an easy feat. If you're liked by the teachers, students think you're a teacher's pet. If you are liked by all the students, the teachers find it suspicious. They think you're the one who'll lead the rebellion. Labelling him as a popular jock would be insulting him. He was even more than a social butterfly. He was a flower and other flocked around him like bees. A pretty boy with a pretty weird personality is what he is. His answers never had been predictable. Cove was the description of thinking outside the box. Heck, he never stepped into the box to begin with. With my description, you might think him the clown of the school. He was no such thing. He didn't even need to try and people laughed at his words. Back then, I caught myself hiding a laugh behind a book a few times when overhearing one of his jokes. My eyes followed his itinerary with cautious. To see him was shocking, but the fact that it's in a library stupefied me. It's the last place my subconscious would imagine us meeting. During the entirety of my career as a student, I've never seen him holding a book, even manuals; he'd magically forget them every time and receive multiple offers from classmates to share theirs. I genuinely thought I'd never see him again following our graduation. He attended a nice college in a city more sophisticated while I attended a local college. I never left town while he must have visited the world with friends during his breaks. Was he feeling sentimental and decided to walk down memory lane? This act of surprise on my part had only lasted a couple of minutes before my reflex to hide came. It would be awkward to meet after so long. We weren't close; I don't even recall any interactions we had. If he wants to check out his books, Ms. Elgnis is available. I hid behind a bookshelf even I was unlikely to be at: the history section.

Chapter 2

"What might you be doing, miss Salem?"

I turned instantly, receiving the biggest shock of my life. Ms. Elgnis stood in front of me, blinking rapidly.

"Did I scare you?" she laughed. "Have I caught you looking at something inappropriate?"

"No, no," I quickly replied, patting down the bottom of my dress. "I noticed dust on these shelves from afar and came to verify."

"You dusted the shelves yesterday, Salem," she remarked.

"Did I? I don't recall. I must be growing old," I said, laughing the second after.

Throwing such remarks in a jokingly manner is a routine for us. It only showed how close we were.

"Hilarious." Ms. Elgnis set her hand on her

hips and lowered her eyes at me, then a smile crept on her plum face. "There's a guy who's going to check out his books soon. Could you take care of him? I need to check the inventory," she asked, already walking away.

She didn't wait for my answer, as she saw no reason for me to refuse. There shouldn't be any reason. There never were until freaking Cove Evaw walked in Glass Wing. Ms. Elgnis had entered the back room and I now know that I can't hide anymore. For this day only, I wished we had installed those job stealing machines—just one. By chance, I hoped he would fail to remember me. I hoped he'd see me as a young librarian who's going to help him check his books out. The chances of that happening were low, but still there. I wasn't very noticeable back in high school. I was a loner and my hair colour differed from now. A couple of months ago, I dyed it olive-green because of a book character. That hair colour sounded as nice as it looked. With the sensation of ants crawling on my feet, I walked to my station. Behind my desk, I could see him approaching. Strings tugged my heart, and I was near the vomiting point. Thank the stars his eyes were glued to the books he carried.

They were graphic novels. That's what he came for. It explains a lot. Still, it's an improvement since there are words on the drawings. The nearer he got, the more I lowered my eyes, hoping we wouldn't have to match eyes. Let's scan the items and let him go. I don't need to be on my best behaviour today. Let him think I have no manners and can't even greet a visitor. Let him think whatever he wants about a stranger. Yes, a stranger, that's what I want to be for him.

"Hello, I'd like to check out these books." I jumped. His voice was more silvery than I'd remember; clear, light and pleasant to the ear.

Desperate times required desperate measures; without looking up or muttering a word, I took his books.

"May I have your card?" this, I had to say. I spoke in a lower tone, fully knowing that my voice was the last thing he'd remember, having barely heard it.

"I don't have a library card." I forgot about this little yet significant detail.

In the end, I lifted my head. This was going to be a meticulous process and changing my voice while staring at volumes of 'One Piece' wouldn't allow me to handle it correctly.

"Would you like to make a card? It's the only way to borrow books from the library."

He furrowed his eyebrows and squinted his eyes at me. Was our policy too harsh for his liking?

"Wait a minute," he said. "I know you," *please say you don't,* "you're Salem!"

Recognizing me is one thing but my name? How? Even in high school, most people didn't know my name. Each time they'd need something, they'd start with: "What was your name again?" then they'd squint, pretending the answer was on the tip of their tongue until I'd say it myself. "Ah yes, Salem!" No wonder he was loved by everyone. Was this all done on purpose? Did he steal the name sheets and intensely studied it till three in the morning, on the first day? This image of best boy might have been all his master plan. Don't mind my overflowing imagination.

"We used to go to school together," he continued. His face lightened up like the sun, his brown eyes emitting the rays and his long smile, the warmth.

"We did, didn't we..." the enthusiasm screamed to be let out of the box.

"Hey, you changed your hair!" Again with

the surprises.

How'd he remember my hair? In addition, the olive-green had started to fade. I didn't make a follow up appointment since I knew my liking of this colour would be short-lived.

"You didn't change yours," is the lame reply I took out of my colourful mind.

"No, I didn't. Should I?" he said in a tone I couldn't decipher. His eyes had a sparkle to them and the corner of his lips were raised. Correction, they were fixed in that position.

Nothing changed about him. He's still the weird guy I used to know. Did I really know him?

"You should do what you want," I said, my answer as dry as bread without a glass of milk.

"I've always wanted to hear these words. You're the first to tell me that." It sounded comic, while for an odd reason, it almost felt sad.

"Would you still like the card?" I asked.

"Definitely!"

"Then you need to fill out a form."

I shifted my body towards the computer to print out a library card request form. It wasn't so common to get new readers and thus printing some in advance with no guarantee would only be a waste of paper. Cove took the liberty to keep talking while I looked for the folder containing the form.

"While I'm not surprised to see you working here, I am." What was that even supposed to mean? "I knew you loved reading, but to this extent, no," he quickly corrected himself. "Don't get me wrong, it's pretty cool." Yeah, right, like it'd believe that. He probably thinks that I'm slowly turning into a cat lady, except with books as my babies. I've heard it all before.

I took the warm sheet of paper and handed it to him along with a ball-point pen that laid on the desk.

"It's simple. Fill in the appropriate cases with your full name, date of birth, phone number and address. You'll receive your card in the mail in the next couple of days."

"Can I come pick it up here?"

"If you'd like."

He clicked the pen and stopped talking for a second, pleasing my ears in the process. A quiet library; that's what this place is supposed to be.

"Aren't you curious to know why I am here? In this town? After all this time." He emphasized words like a kid and was this close to use hand gestures. And all this time was merely three years, yet he talks like it's been thirty.

My silence was his answer because he looked at me, blinking his eyes like an innocent child. With the exception that there was nothing innocent about this child.

"I'm here on my summer break. Normally I would spend this break with friends elsewhere, but I wasn't feeling it this year. To clear my head, I came back." He had questioned and answered everything by himself. For once he wasn't best boy but pathetic boy.

He handed me back the sheet, and I stayed true to my job. I couldn't care less about his reasons for coming back. In fact, I cared more for today's special at a restaurant I went to twice a year.

"A reminder that the card will be ready in a couple of days. Since you're coming to pick it up, you'll receive a notification via text when it's here. For now, I'll print you a temporary card for you to check out these books."

I kept it professional since all we were now was librarian and guy who wants to borrow his graphic novels. We're no longer classmates.

"Thank you," he said, that smile going nowhere else but on his face. "I have to ask you something." What now? "Whose cat is this?" he said, pointing to Nabi, who rubbed her body against his leg affectionately. She only did that to people she was comfortable with. It took weeks for me. "She's adorable." He held her in his arms and rubbed his face on hers. "She has a collar with a bow, so I'm thinking she has an owner."

"She's the library cat. She came here so often, we adopted her."

"Her name?" I was so brief when I spoke that Cove had to remind me of it each time—in his own way.

"Nabi."

"I've never heard of that name before."

"In a certain country, it's very common."

"Care to explain?"

Maybe I was in the wrong here.

"Nabi in Korean is butterfly—which is my favourite animal. And for an unknown reason, it is very common to call a cat Nabi in Korea."

"Interesting." my short tongue was contagious.

He patted her little head, making Nabi purr

and Cove, melt. Hearts in his eyes and a small smile formed on my face. I couldn't help it. It was human nature.

"I found myself an extra reason to come here again. They keep piling," he said, bringing her back on the carpet. When you talk of a pile, you'd think of many. I'm sure his only reasons are the graphic novels and Nabi. "I'll get going now. It was nice to see you," he said, taking his leave with books at his side and the temporary card document sticking out of the back pocket of his beige cargo shorts.

At last, I could breathe again.

"You betrayed me, Nabi," I told her while she laid on the carpet, not a care in the world.

I pressed her little nose and walked past. One who could be mad at a kitty is without a soul.

Having some work left to do, I decided to forget about what happened. I pretended this day was like any other. When I tried to erase our awkward conversation, the coming days came to mind. Distracting myself with work gave me the peace of mind to think—which in this case was bad. While performing an impromptu and unnecessary inventory of section A to Z, I imagined myself bumping into Cove between shelves. While overseeing the checkout of a few readers, I imagined their 7 faces as Cove's. While creating lists of book recommendations, I thought of books I might be able to convince Cove to read. One meeting turned me insane. I doubt Cove's the only cause. I tend to overly worry about events that have yet to happen; it's in my nature. He scared me by saying he'll come again. My mind drifted without a break to thoughts of future days.

Meanwhile, hours had since passed without prior notice. Time hadn't informed that the pace was going to be different. My shift had ended, and I stayed in the library, as always. I didn't do it for over-time but to be a visitor with a library card of my own. I moved to my favourite spot, the border of a large window. We'd put pillows there to sit. I stay there with a book and Nabi joins me when it pleases her. The last rays of sunlight for the day hit that corner, passing by Nabi. It reflected on her short black fur and was warm to the touch. Her green eyes resembled two peridot stones when under the sun. This is the moment I look forward to every day. Not even Cove could destroy it. Once I unlock the door presented to me by the book in my hands, I enter another universe. Reading is my pocket sized solution to problems. It fights off most of them, effortlessly. It's my saviour and addiction.

Chapter 3

Placing a few strawberries on the cutting board, I took my time in observing them. I always liked to notice how cute the little ones were and how plum the bigger ones were. Eating a tiny one, the taste of fresh strawberries waltzed in me. When the sweetness hit the surface of my tongue, my feet start the happy dance. The strawberries grown in Mardi Town were the best I knew. At times, I'd find some packs at the grocery story imported from different towns or countries; I tried them out of curiosity. The results were... as expected. After all that silliness, I roll up my sleeves and start the labour—or so I thought. Wanting to portray the lines inside the strawberries, I cut them carefully in half. Cutting them this way won't make it easier for the mixer, it's merely to treat my eyes. Plucking the leaves out, I recalled the time I attempted to blend in the leaves along with the strawberry milk. It was so bitter I had to throw it out, wasting fresh strawberries. I know now to keep putting the leaves in the compost where they'll be off to a better place. With a wooden spoon, I added honey to make it even sweeter. They say metal removes the nutrients from honey, hence my usage of a wooden spoon. I have no clue whether any of this is true. It's knowledge that was passed on by word of mouth. Take is with a grain of salt. I've now made enough strawberry milk to last three days, any more and it'll rot, any less and I'll be too bothered to make it again so soon. No matter how much I drink, I can never get sick of this special milk. My first encounter with it was at a coffee shop on Cherry Street. They were handing out free samples. One sip and I was hooked—for life, it seems. Now for my only source of exercise, a daily night walk. My house was near the Lupin lake which was on the nature side of Mardi Town, and walking alone at night isn't a problem. It's pretty quiet and empty unless the night market opened and that only happens once a week. To counterbalance the cool weather, I wore a sweatshirt that just happened to match the colour of the night sky. Under I wore a loose and long brown skirt. For the finishing touch, a foliage fabric headband—another one of my obsession. I have plenty of them in a hatbox under my bed. New kinds of fabric show up all the time at the market and it's hard to resist. There's another market in this part of town, the morning market. This one happens daily, but it starts quite early, earlier than my alarm time. I end up going on the weekend for my headbands. I purchase square pieces of fabric —normally used as handkerchiefs—fold them diagonally, then in half. Pinching the ends, I proceed to put my hair up in a ponytail and wrap the fabric around my head. Following that, I tie loose ends. The last step is to double knot the ends in order to have an adorable bow. It's comfortable as well as neat. It makes me feel good to have a certain point in my outfit. Fashion wasn't my forte. I chose what pleased my fickle eyes and that was it.

"Don't stay out too late," my mother said from the kitchen table as she typed away on her laptop, glasses on her eyes that protected her from the blue light. My mother's an anthropologist, a very passionate one at that.

Work is fun for her and fun is work. There can never be too much fun, right?

"I won't," I answered before closing and locking the door on my way out. I still lived with my parents because it would be a waste to pay rent for an apartment when I practically lived in the library. My room's only utility is to give me a good night's rest. Even now, I'm on my way to Glass Wing; the walk's only a pretense. Nonetheless, I help out cost-wise at home since I'm of age and earn a paycheck. Now let's head to the library. I am well aware of the closing time but I'm an employee and there's no rule against my presence there at such a time—at least, not to my knowledge, the Glass Wing manual is the only book I failed to read whole. Each time of the day has its charms. The night is dark and peaceful, perfect to cozy up in a corner with a book. A dream of mine is to permanently live in the library, to experience every single moment there. Imagine having a catalogue of books to choose from for bedtime. And imagine holding a sweet drink in one hand, a book in the other while sitting at the edge of the window, having the moon in your range of vision. I don't exactly need to imagine this one since I'm on my way to do exactly that. The only problem is the fact I can't stay late. The glass slippers and the pumpkin carriage disappear at midnight. I'll take any opportunity I get to reference a tale. Although I chose my two legs for transportation, it still took no time. The library's at a good walking distance, just as it is at a suitable distance for a bike. Alas, I'd stopped in my tracks. A terrifying sight forced me to halt. The absence of light made it hard to discern. But with my 2.0 vision, I could see the figure of a man lurking near the library. When I took a step back, he took one ahead. The dark silhouette turned to a familiar one. I now feared it even more. How unexpected to see Cove, again, at the library and at this hour.

 "Salem, is that you?" he said, emerging from the darkness.

"What are you doing here?" Had I always been so cold towards people?

He scratched the back of his head and gazed at me with droopy eyes, "I was wondering if the library was still open?"

"How could it be? Look at the sky."

"I had a glimmer of a hope, turns out it wasn't enough."

 Even in the breezy weather, he kept his cargo

shorts on, though he changed his tee to a mint-coloured sweatshirt. I guess his legs tend to stay warm on their own. I'm jealous of that and rued the choice of having worn a skirt. It covered my legs but left the wind an entrance from the bottom.

"Did you need something from the library?" the librarian in me spoke.

"It's strange. I finished those all the books I borrowed, it was only a couple of them, but I never thought I'd read them all on the same day. And I'm dying to know what happens in the next volume."

Unknowingly, I smiled. This feeling he has is oh-so familiar to me. Experiencing it for the first time must be magic. In a sense, I felt proud. I'd be even more if he picked up some novels as well.

He continued, "You think you could let me borrow some, in secret?" his voice had turned into a whisper, which was useless since no one stood in our surroundings.

My heart was crushed, and I'd suddenly wanted to accept his cautiously asked request.

I played along by whispering, "You're in luck. I was going there too."

His face lit up—it tends to do that.

"You were? Fate brought us here, don't you think?"

That's it. My smile was wiped off after hearing those foam-like words. Fate is fiction. It's something for the books.

"Let's go inside," I said, my words coming out of the mouth of a desert.

"Aye, aye, captain!"

The minute I opened the back door, we were hit by a series of cries. Nabi was next to the door, waving her paws in the air. It's possible she heard us talking outside and got excited. She'd been patiently waiting for a while now; her joy could no longer be contained. Someone else's joy is out of control. Cove threw himself on the ground to rejoice with her. He made weird noised in a very high tone. He spoke an alien language foreign to aliens themselves. It's hard to explain in coherent words and not worth trying. I would only make a fool of myself, much like he is at the present moment. Wasn't he even embarrassed at all? Won't he catch my eye, realize and stand up at the speed of lightning with a flushed face? No, when he did look at me, there was no change in his expression. Life must be good when you can easily show your true self to anyone. As an introvert, I can't relate.

"Um," I said, making him turn his head to face me.

His back was on the ground while he lifted Nabi in the air.

"Didn't you need your books?"

"Yes, yes, I'm getting them right now. If I stay too long, I might get you in trouble." He patted Nabi one last time before standing back up.

"It's fine, but this time, take many books at once."

"Maybe, maybe not," he said, a sheepish expression on him.

The meaning behind his words were hidden in Pandora's box along with secrets we're better off not knowing. This specific box was made to remain closed; let's respect its purpose. Without a second to waste, cove ran off to the graphic novels' section where the shelves were shorter. This old fashion town had only recently hopped on the wagon. I admit, they're not so bad. I gobbled up a few in a single sitting. You can even spot some decent quotes in the midst of the countless drawings. I stood and watched for a while, a happy Cove searching for his volumes and flipping through a couple of pages. Why would he do that? Was he planning on reading them here?

As I thought about it, he came to me, his eyes rounder than before.

"I need to ask you why you came here at night. You asked me earlier, and I answered. It's only fair for you to do the same."

I gulped; the question was easy, but it made me nervous. Why? I don't know.

"To read, what else?"

"That means you're staying here longer. Right?" He tilted his head, and I almost saw fluffy ears appearing on his head.

I tried to ignore him, since I knew what he meant. He didn't need to add any more words for me to understand he wanted to read here. It was no use arguing. He's not the type to let go of something—that I remember.

"Alright, you can stay. We won't get in trouble. I come here every night."

The last part maybe I shouldn't have added. He nodded and then went back to his pile of books. I myself had found a book. To say found would be lying since I hid it in the drawer of my station. This wasn't an act of fair play, but this book was worth the stain on my conscience. And so I read. Well, I tried to, but one way or another, my eyes constantly went to Cove. I was mad that he'd stolen my spot at the edge of the window. That's where I wanted to read. Now I'm stuck at my station. And there's a traitor between us. I'm talking about Nabi. She sat in front of him, taking the remaining spot. With both of them there, I could not fit, nor did I want to attempt it. I opened my book without success. The words hadn't made me dream.

Chapter 4

The first phrase of my page was: *Thunder struck*. I wished that happened here. For the first time in my life, the silence inside the library was unbearable. It was deafening. I read page after page, understanding nothing. I don't recall what I've read. I could have read an explicit novel by accident and wouldn't have realized it. My focus was lost. This was a once in a blue moon event. My mind was somewhere else, on the elephant in the room. Contrary to me, his eyes were glued to the pages as he flipped at full throttle. I could not comprehend why he was a distraction. The lack of people as well as the hour must be adding to it. He alone could not have such powers. I blame the other factors. Blaming didn't help my cause; it never did for anyone. I fought it off and dived headfirst into the book I held with utmost care. In the matter of minutes, I'd even start to take notice of the ticking sound from the clock. When I first came to the library, that sound was noticeable as I was nervous in an unfamiliar environment. After days and weeks, it slowly went unnoticed, but today... It came back ringing in my ears like an attention-seeker. What's wrong with me?

"Something wrong?" Cove asked from afar, making me jump.

He hadn't caught me staring since I hadn't, but I wondered if he'd read my mind instead. I don't know which is worse.

"There's nothing."

He had turned naughty—in a playful way. He was close to a laugh. I had to stop it before it came out.

"I thought you came here to read. Am I making you uncomfortable?" he said, the laughter being suppressed some more.

What would he laugh about? What was so funny? I surrendered to my thoughts and asked him directly. Though his answer took me aback, it stupefied me.

"Because I like you," he said.

I looked at him, thinking he was crazy. He

most probably was. I read an immense number of books in this library, but none taught me how to deal with this kind of situation. What even was this situation?

"You don't believe me?" he asked.

"I don't." It had to be a joke.

"I really do. You might have not noticed it in high school since you gave your full attention to books, but it's true that you've always caught my eye. Today, I saw you couldn't give that full attention to a book and so I tested my luck."

He kept on explaining himself while I stayed quiet, not knowing how to react. Luck, he said; it made no sense. Even when talking, he showed no signs of being nervous, which you usually are when confessing. His words were coherent, there was no stuttering. His skin was neither pale nor soaked, pupils were stable and overall, his posture was relaxed— his legs were crossed on the edge of the window, looking like the main character of an anime.

He concluded with: "What do you think?"

Before answering, I took a profound breath. That smile, that near laugh and that unexpected confession were all accomplices in the mission to make me doubt his intentions. I could only doubt words coming out of a boy I knew to never be serious. Cove is the boy who cried wolf. I wasn't too concern on how to answer. Whether it was a joke or the truth, my answer won't embarrass me.

Clearly, I told him: "It's not reciprocate."

The measly feelings I had for him back in high school were long gone. In the small society that was high school, interesting people were very few. It's a tradition to have small insignificant crushes. That's what he was for me, a crush. If currently, he wasn't joking, that's also what I might have been for him, a crush. Seeing me now may have ignited the flame, but that's an illusion. Wake up, Cove, you don't genuinely like me...is what I wanted to tell him, but that'll sound too conceited of me. I don't want to sound like anything. I don't want to make a mark on his mind or any other. I don't want to remain in the memories of someone. Solitude suits me.

"I don't feel the same as you and if you have all your books, it'd be best to check them out for us to go back home. It's getting late."

"Were you always this cold?" when he said that, I expected him to look at me with frustration, but his eyes were as loving as could be.

Words I should have been offended by turned soft, flustering me. Was it because his tone matched the look in his eyes? He came over with merely two books in hand.

"Didn't you say you read them fast?"

"A few hours won't kill me. I'll come back tomorrow, the day after and the other days that follow." That smile never faded; the moment it does, it'll be quite the fright. "You'll be seeing me around," he said, handing me the books.

Since the machines were off and turning them on would leave a trace of our secret meeting, I checked them out manually. The traditional way with little papers you'd slip into a pocket glued inside the book. You'd write the borrower's name, today's date and the due date. And in the library's record, you'd write the same information. Alas, today, it seems I'll break the rule and write it in my own records—a notepad filled with cat stickers. If he returns the books quickly, I won't need to add it to the official records and we could all pretend that this night never happened. How I wished it never did. If I had avoided him properly in the morning, if I held on to Ms. Elgnis; my upcoming days would have been saved. Sadly, no vortex will come to eat this portion of time. That only happens in novels. My opinion on Neverland is changing. If Peter Pan asks me to go there, perhaps I'll go to the land where all I imagine comes true.

"Thank you for the books, Salem. We'll see each other in the morning, maybe the afternoon, or maybe even the night."

I frowned at him, thinking he'll never be welcome in the library when the sun's down. If I had the authority, he wouldn't even be allowed when the sun's up either.

Unfortunately, the sun rose and along tagged Cove. He came in Glass Wing wearing a purple jersey, the number five drawn on the back in red. I've seen that top before, quite often. He was part of the track team in high school. Whilst walking in the hallway, by the window, I caught glimpses of Cove running on the tracks. He'd never missed a single day. That grabbed my attention. He ran as if he were chased by debt collectors. Three years had gone by since and he looked the same for the exception of the hair strands on his head that usually were drenched in sweat and his cheeks that were red like strawberries. I assume he stopped running after going off to college. The Cove I knew would have run to the library, using it as an excuse to practice. It's a shame he'd stopped. He looked the happiest when running. Maybe that's why I felt something was missing even though he smiled.

"Ahoy, Salem Matey!" he said to me, having read pirate books.

"Ahoy," I replied, my soul leaving my body.

He must have been pleasantly surprised to see me play along—it's hard to hide my own love for pirates. His smile was of a five-year-old.

"At least I now know you don't hate me," he said, nudging my shoulder.

"It's my job to play along with the children who come to read," I replied, walking away.

He held on to his heart, pretending to be hurt, and then he trailed behind me like the child he is.

"Laugh at me all you want Salem, that won't change a thing."

I abruptly stepped on the brakes, causing him to bump with my back. When turning around, Cove hadn't stepped back. He stood so close to me, I could notice everything—mostly his clean baby scent, it was soft and lily-like. No hint of perfume; I don't think he uses any. It's so natural yet makes me wonder how raw skin could smell this way? And how could it be so distracting?

"Could you stop following me?" I said, regaining my senses. "I have work to do while you need to return to doing whatever you need to do. Don't waste your summer by spending it in a library."

The irony of my words. I advocated the hobby of reading. I brought in new readers with any ways I found under my sleeve. That day, I'd rid myself of the sleeves. Still, It wasn't enough. For him, my words were lighter than my tolerance towards alcohol. Cove dropped by day after day, wearing either his jersey with matching running shorts or a various selection of tees with his beige cargo pants. He'd follow me till I arrived at the back room and get the door slammed on his nose. He'd switch out books I'd just organized, making me stay at the same shelf for longer than intended. He'd sit near the window and monopolize the time one could spend with Nabi. If I'd want to see her, the only way is to sit close to him. As hard as it was, I fought the urge and haven't given in.

He's bored out of his skull to be messing with me. Was that the reaction of someone having faced a rejection? Was this a revenge or a scheme to change my mind? I believed nothing of what I'd just thought. His confession didn't seem real. Cove was messing with my head in ways I couldn't understand. Where have my peaceful summer days gone to?

After days of torture, I had the inkling of a solution in mind. It was complex and required planning and so I did it. I was crossed legged on the fluffy carpet on the floor of my bedroom, aka the only place I am safe from Cove. Then I proceeded to waste a sheet of paper writing down my plan to get Cove away from me. At this hour, I could have been reading a good book but no, I have to use my precious time, a sheet of paper that was better off staying blank in the deep end of my drawer and the fresh ink of a pen I had yet to use.

Step 1. Discreetly bring up the idea of "the distraction".

In this case, the distraction is my bright idea—the only one I could come up with—books. There is no turning back when you get lost in the world of books. There is a way in, but there's no exit. I figured that if he fell in love with books, he'd fall out of love with me. This world world will be more captivating than mine.

Step 2. Convince the subject.

Cove is merely a subject in this confidential operation. And this subject reads books with a word count equivalent to a single novel chapter. For people like him, seeing the thickness of the book will intimidate him. Let's not talk about the pages filled with words. For a visual person, it does seem like quite the task. All because he doesn't know the charm of getting thrown into a story with only the narrator as a safety handle or the bliss from emotions being sent on a one-way road to your heart. Books are my personal vending machine of feelings. I feel through books more than I do in real life.

Step 3. Prepare a list of books well suited for the subject.

Picking out books outside of your box of interests doesn't do you any good. It's a given to find reading boring if you choose books that will make you look good but haven't piqued your interest. For Cove, I'll pick them out for him. Knowing him, he'd never look past the graphic novel shelf. Even when he followed me around, he didn't linger on a certain shelf to read the blurb of a book that looked entertaining. Besides, it was part of my job to make reading lists; I can create them in my sleep. Cove. Be prepared for your heart to go in a completely different direction. I'll make a bookworm out of you.

Chapter 5

"Your prince charming isn't here yet. That's odd," Ms. Elgnis said, holding a book in her hand—she pretended to read but she was all ears for gossip.

A librarian is always ready to hear stories even if they're not from fiction pieces.

"He's not my prince charming," I replied, not wasting the second of a breath.

"As if," she said, slamming shut her book. "He's following you around like a puppy and those eyes, endearment is written all over them."

"There's nothing going on."

"Give him a chance and bring some romance into your life."

I wanted to let out a laugh so loud it'll wake the hibernating bears, but I resisted.

"I have all the romance I need," I said,

pointing at the shelf next to me that just happened to be the new adult romance one.

"Aren't you tired of hearing the love story of others? Don't you want to experience your own?" Ms. Elgnis crossed her arms, wrinkling part of her flowery dress.

"I read plenty of books written from a first person's point of view. I've experienced things grander than love this way."

"Is there such a thing?" she remarked, "Love is as grand as it gets." Ms. Elgnis put on a smile that, to me, looked painful.

She hadn't had the best luck in love, bringing her to live alone at such an age. She never was able to settle down with a man. Something always happened prior to the wedding. Life happened in various fashions, and the cause of separation wasn't always a fault. She once told me that time could be a factor for separation. And people who still loved each other could make such a call, each time for a different reason. In the end, they'll remember one another. *That's Amore!* She told me. I don't get it and at this rate, I never will. Love in books is more straightforward and less complicated. It does start with difficulties, goes downhill the moment it got better, but in the end, they get together. It's a happy ending.

"It's not for me," I said, having no clue of my motive.

Why wasn't love for me? Could a human being live without it? Could you live off books?

"Suit yourself then, but don't let him hanging too long. Even cute puppy-like guys get tired and look somewhere else. The puppy becomes a dog."

"Let him go somewhere else. I'm sure he's only having fun with me."

Ms. Elgnis laughed her way out of the library to take her break, the bottom of her wide-legged pants flying up from the wind coming of her strides.

Meanwhile, I'd found something that was grander than the love Ms. Elgnis talked of: someone caught red-handed. On my desk, a black kitten bleeped out her tongue to reach the strawberry milk in my porcelain cup. She'd caught my eye and ignored it.

"Strawberries are too sweet for cats, Nabi," I told her, snatching the cup away.

I held it in my hands since however high I positioned it, Nabi and her agility would reach it in the blink of an eye. She could climb on me to get another lick of the strawberry milk, but I had something those shelves and tables didn't have; two legs to constantly move around. She could follow me all she wants and the only thing she'd get was a pat on the head. I drank my milk in one go, not wanting to wander around with a cup in my hand. What if I spilled it on a book? I'd hold myself accountable for the rest of my days. Drinks aside, it's here, the storm ravaging through my peaceful life. Cove walked in, his smile reaching his ears. I turned away only then to match eyes with a snickering Ms. Elgnis. She hid her mouth with a book, but it was too late.

Though I'd planned out my proposition, seeing him reminded me that this plan could seem laughable. Hearing him laugh at me was the last thing I'd want to hear. I barely slept last night, because of this plan. I'd spend hours making this Cove reading list. I needed to find short books for him to not sigh at the sight of a huge block of paper. In reality, length doesn't matter if you are immersed in the story. Again, I needed to get down to Cove's level. Small steps first. Regardless of length, short books can be just as good while long books can be just as bad. Vice-versa. Every storyteller tells their story differently at their own pace. Thus, this reading list is filled with short books of quality. The other dilemma was to match his preferences. This plan is as good as garbage if I'd chosen well-known books that Cove doesn't find interesting. That is the charm of books, the fact that the judging of a book can only be done in a subjective manner. You may like a book your neighbour despises. A book can never be bad or good to everyone. It's art sold at a lower price and distributed widely. Still, despite the difficulties, I managed to make that list. I had used that sheet as a bookmark for the book Peter Pan that just happened to be included. Think about it, he likes pirates and the sea and the book on my night stand was all about that; Hook and his crew, the Neverland island. Plus, Cove gave me the impression of a lost child. This tale might help him grow up and find his road. I hope he doesn't do the opposite and makes Peter his role model. Kids, it's Wendy who's wiser. The second book on the list is a novel called the hidden time; it's more recent and has been published independently. It is about pirates who are afraid that their traditions would become lost in time. The solution they came up with was a time capsule disguised as a hidden treasure.

They hope the newer generations of pirates find it in the future. Throughout the novel and their journey, they find meaning behind every object they decide to leave in the capsule. They wonder about which traditions should be kept and which should be forgotten. I personally thought the message behind this book can also be used in modern times. And I wonder if Cove will find the hidden message. Next on the list is Robinson Crusoe. It's a pretty famous novel that doesn't require to be explained. Let's just say it has something to do with an island and automatically the sea. We can move on to the final book, the cherry on top, Aesop's fables. My motive is a bit comical. Aesop is an old story teller and in the graphic novel Cove is reading there is a character with an extremely similar name; coincidentally, he tells many stories (lies). To give him fables might be a little childish seeing that each one is the length of a paragraph. However, they do hold important morals. This book could be the one who'll turn him into a good person. I'm sure he'll be thankful to see the length of this one. That is, if I muster the courage to give him the list. If the plan is successful, I'll be alone and he'll need a scroll to write out all the books he'd want to read. Now here it came—the moment I'd need to explain this mess of a plan.

Subject locked on radar. Shoot!

"Looking lovely today Salem with your sea shells printed dress."

Vomit locked on radar. Suppress!

"Hello, Cove," I smiled, as if my life depended on it. It did.

"Something changed about you," he said, taking a step back to look me up and down.

I must have not greeted him properly in the past few days for him to say that.

"Nothing's changed, yet!" My smile turned into a laugh. A villain's laugh—am introverted one.

"Should I worry about this?" he said, looking around as if a crowd were witnessing our scene.

"Cove, I have a proposition for you. A challenge, to be more precise."

The moment he heard the word challenge, he perked up. He hasn't changed, he is still the competitive person I knew him to be. If I don't use this word, there isn't much I can do to convince him. The word 'challenge' is my hidden card. Using his pride for my own gains, evil, I know. Well, not-so-evil if you think about it. He'll get some knowledge out of it and a clearer mind. I'm not the person he should like.

"I see you reading graphic novels every day, but have you thought of novels?"

His sly smile turned into a frown and though I expected it; I panicked and blabbered off script.

"I prepared a list for you." Not my best try.

"Why would I read boring blocks of papers?"

This was on my list of Cove-like answers.

"Don't think of them this way. They draw pictures in your mind, they're colourful. As you read, you imagine how the characters look like, their expressions, the world they live in and what they use. It's magical."

"Books are lucky," he said in response.

Now this wasn't on my list of Cove-like answers.

"They are?"

"You were never this talkative. I've only heard a couple of words from you during our teenage years. When it comes to books, the motor in your mouth activates."

Motor? For some reason, this word offended me.

"Are you saying that I talked too much?"

"Not at all. I could hear you talk all day." He shook his head, and spoke so very slowly it made something shift in my stomach.

"Returning to my proposition," I coughed. "Would you accept the challenge? You must be bored coming here every single day. Tell you what, I give you till the end of your summer to finish all the books on the list. Then you can prove there's really nothing you can't do."

I hit where it hurts with poison and ended with flattery as the medicine.

"I'll agree if you take on a challenge. It's only fair if you do too," he said, crossing his arms, creasing his shirt. It was a challenge to find the new crease in the midst of so many.

"What kind of challenge?"

There was no time to fear the worst, and so I didn't.

"You'd have to go on dates with me during the same time period you gave me."

Seeing the disgust on my face, he quickly changed his words.

"Friendly dates. You see, all my friends are somewhere else in the world and besides from my parents, you are the only one I know here in town. Well, there are others from high school, but the ones left were never very likeable. You are the only one." He looked at me, a pleading look to his eyes and a protruding lower lip. "I want to have fun on my break. It's not fun to be lonely. If you accept the couple of *friendly* dates, I'll leave you alone and still read all the books on the list."

"How many friendly dates are we talking about?"

I do realize accepting his offer would be counterproductive. Reading would give him less time to follow me around, but going out with him makes me voluntarily spend time with him, which is the last thing I'd thought I'd do. On the bright side—yes, there is one—he did say he'd leave me alone. I've always heard good things take time. I believe in this fetish sentence.

At the same time, Cove tilted his head from right to left. This sight made me want to go easy on him and accept any numbers he'd throw in my way. On second thoughts, it will never happen. I need to bargain. This was quite the bittersweet day.

Crippling his fingers, he opened his mouth to at last say a number:

"20, my lucky number."

"That's too much," it really was.

"It is? 19 then."

"You've only dropped it by one. It's not enough."

"19 is already very low. How much do you want to drop it to? Don't tell me zero because I'm dead serious."

I'd be dead serious too if I'd said zero. Trust me, the urge to say zero had almost reached its limit.

A man with golden locks and brownish eyes stared at me, waiting for an answer that'll possibly determine his upcoming days. It was tough.

I pulled through eventually.

"15! That's my final offer," I said, biting my lip.

"I was the one doing the offers, but okay, I'll take you on for 15. We have a deal!"

He reached a hand for a high five and I hit it; images of peaceful summer days flashing before my eyes.

Chapter 6

Cove's point of view

Like in the movies, a flyer taken by the wind landed on my face. Why would you ruin a beautiful day? Someone tell me why? Removing it, I saw words printed in bright red that triggered me. I'd never wanted to see those words again. These past few years, I did my best to avoid them and the minute I come back; they come looking for me themselves. Some people would call it fate. I call it a curse. The star in me had already dimmed until it died. Attempting to revive it would be useless. The flyer had read: Recruiting for the track team of Mardi Town. It's an opportunity I longed for in my younger years. Now I turn a blind eye to it. In me rose anger and a hit of sadness; a sensation familiar to me. The world seems sombre and so small.

Crumpling the paper into a ball, it threw it in the nearest garbage. My day had started with excitement. It's a shame it turned out this way. Seeing her face will probably clear the grey clouds in my sky and chase away the rain. Entering Glass Wing, she's the first one I saw. My eyes go directly to her, like instincts. Her olive green hair was put behind her ear and she wore a pretty unique dress. It was long and covered by vintage clock motifs. The cutest point was the socks sticking out of her white sneakers; little strawberries were drawn on them. I can see she found her style, summer dresses and cute socks. She's changed quite a bit. In her was this newly found leisure. It's like she's been freed. She embodies the librarian look with perfection. If there was a librarian this pretty when I was younger, maybe I'd visited this place. It's never too late, no? All that to say that she's gained comfort. She's in her element and glowed with adoration for it. I admired this side of hers as much as I envied it. If only I could love an occupation like her. To have hearts in my eyes and a fire burning when speaking of it. During my studies, I wasn't lucky enough for that.

There were no sparks in me. None. On the contrary, it's a pain to study something so far from my interests. I rode the wave my classmates picked and later was engulfed by it. And to clear my mind, I came back to my hometown. By the end of my break, I hope for my compass to regain a sense of direction. Now, I'd need to focus on the fact I stood in the same place as Salem, hoping I don't blow it this time.

"Good morning! We have a date after work," I told her. Bringing her attention out of the book she read standing next to a shelf.

Only when those words came out of my mouth could I believe I was going on a date with Salem. Saying that I meticulously planned those fifteen outings last night would be a lie. A big fat lie. I'm not the type to organize. I let it flow. This very day seemed perfect for a date, so it's decided.

"I'd rather you call it a friendly outing but, good morning." She said, her voice sounding like calm waters after a storm.

"You could have a date with a family member or a friend. I think it's fine to call it a date."

"It's not fine in my book," she said,

breaking my heart.

Then again, what am I If not stubborn?

"See you on our date."

Flashing a smile, I let her back to her duties and went to my other crush, sweet little Nabi. I've always loved cats. There are two cats in my house—Lou and Mari—that I missed dearly when I was in college. Meeting Nabi was yet another bliss. A destructive one. When I come home from the library, my cats, with their highly developed little noses, can sniff the foreign cat on me. They hiss and avoid me until I take a shower and wear clothing with only their fur stuck to it. I didn't raise them this way. Then again, cats have a mind of their own. You can't really raise or train them like you'd do with dogs.

Little Nabi sat on my lap, leaving me conflicted. I'd taken a seat near the window without having taken out a single book. I couldn't disturb a kitten, but I needed to start Salem's challenge. What to do, really? The odds of Nabi coming back to me if I stood are low. Cats are fickle creatures. She might like me now and want nothing to do with me the next minute. In this extensive library, I'm sure she has tons of favourite places to rest. Were it not for Salem, I'd stay with Nabi over any book. From my bag, I took out a copy of Peter Pan; Salem handed it to me the previous day. I removed the paper sticking out of it and laughed a little. She wouldn't need to sign her name to know it's hers. The sheet was decorated with a frame of strawberries, all had smiley faces. Salem is much cuter than she wants us to believe. From her clothes to her favourite motifs, her taste and that smile... She hasn't shown me a smile since I came back to Mardi Town. I'd seen it years back. It was blinding, made me lose sight of the rest. I wish she'd show me the smile she's shown to everyone else but me. Salem is kind to others, while for me... No, actually, she's been nothing but kind. When I followed her around, she let me. Someone else would have cursed and kicked me out of the establishment. I should either have been on a blacklist or the police station for stalking charges. That would be going to the extremes; then again, that would be someone other than Salem. She's kind, too much, actually.

Returning to the list, the first name wasn't foreign to me, but I questioned that choice. I'm too old for Peter Pan. I know that I am at a beginner level for reading but not at children level. I wanted to protest and demand a change in the list. Fables, even more childish and comic—Aesop. Settling down, I guess I'd better trust the judgment of a capable librarian. It shows; her love for books and the knowledge that comes with it.

I started with Peter Pan; it being the first book I received. I'll get to the rest in due time. My back hit the wall and my legs were crossed on the platform, glued to the window. I dreaded the moment where I'd have to open the book and read the black text on white pages. Lines and lines stared at me, intimidating me. A page was enough for my patience to face a crisis and my mind to go blank. This is the first hurdle, one of many. Some say that the beginning is the half of every action, I don't know if I can believe that right now. While I read, my internal voice sounded awkward. I wanted to hear the narrator's voice and the characters; however I'm afraid I wasn't in deep enough. My mind was still on the surface; it floated as if it wore a life jacket. I kept on for the challenge. With time, maybe the jacket will unfasten itself and I'll reach a trench on the seafloor. There is an easy way out—a submarine. One could look up a summary of each chapter online as I did for school, but I wouldn't be proud of it. For school, I hadn't cared enough to feel regretful or to feel it was not a genuine win. Somehow, I cared for this. It's different.

Flipping the page, an image came to me. It may have had something to do with the novel since on this page, they talked about Wendy's mother. I remembered a scene of my own. Years back, during peaceful times where the thought of growth was distant, I sat crossed legs—as I did now—on the carpet of our living room, a game controller in hand. In a corner, my mother sat on a rocking chair, a book in her hands. Each flip of the page entered my ear. It was a favourable background noise, and I purposely turned down the volume of my video game to hear it. Today, it's me who's making that noise. The thought of it brightened the situation. It won't be so bad after all. The more I immersed myself in the story, the more it changed—the voice in my head turned foreign. A storyteller resided in my head and took control. For the first time, I felt out of this world, far from any concerns. Although, it was only a matter of time before I was brought back to earth. Don't get me wrong, the story is far from boring. My attention span is the problem here. It's shorter than the average length of a song. I admit that the book and all its details intrigued me. Peter Pan is a famous tale which I know the story of but obviously, movie adaptations have a time limit and other constraints, thus it can't be the same. It's missing a few elements only found in the book. And it's stimulating to discover those never seen features. Maybe that's why a lot of people prefer the book over the movie. It is the original version. Maybe I was missing out, maybe not. Looking away from the block of paper, I spotted the root of this agony, Salem. I watched as she picked books out of the shelves and placed them into her cart. The clocks on her dress reminded me how the time goes by so slowly in here. It was painfully long to wait for her to call it a day. Salem's here before the library opens and after it closes. Not today, my dear. As soon as the doors are ready to be locked, we'll leave for our date. I deserve the reward after all the reading I did. It may have only been a couple of pages, but hey, it's the effort that counts. Besides, I barely got a shut eye last night thinking of our first date. Even now, as I am sitting in the library, I have no clue to what we'll do once we're out of here. Ideas are floating around and they're all so attractive. I used to be a 'live in the moment' person and now I'm 'what about tomorrow' person. Something changed in me the moment I stepped into another prison with bars looser than the previous. I feel them loosening even more. Who knows, the feet I dipped in the water might find their way at the end of the summer. Alas, today, I still am completely lost, mindless and clueless. Despite having been surrounded by people, loneliness crept in. I felt these interactions weren't genuine. For some time now, my world has been black and white. Help me regain my colours, *Salem*.

Chapter 7

Salem's point of view

All day, my mind wandered. I read pages and understood nothing. Books for me had been blocks of papers today. How could I focus when death awaited me at the end of the day? 'Death' might be an exaggeration. A big one. The word 'death' could be used in various situations; for example: Mine. The death of my free time after work I use for reading or to swing by the Berry Berry farm to stock up on strawberries. It's the death of freedom. Was it too late to cancel the deal? As I drowned in my despair, the cause of it approached me.

"Five minutes until closing time," he said, his lips rising to their spot near his cheekbones.

My response to his comment was a nod, a

reluctant one.

"Let me have these five minutes, then," I pleaded, my sense of humour on the floor.

"As you wish," he said, walking away from me, oddly fast.

Time, couldn't you go by any slower? The day raced its way to the end, making me believe it was now only beginning. Perhaps it was? I'd been lost in my own imaginary world and being taken out of it was scary as hell. Being picked out of the dollhouse and brought into the real world was terrifying. Here came the exaggeration, again. It's a simple outing. A normal one. Normal didn't really fit me, though. I'd never been on a friendly outing, let alone a date. I'm in my twenties and all of my so-called experiences were from books. And I was satisfied with it. People asked me if I wasn't tired of reading about other people's lives while never getting to live myself. I always answered that I lived through books and that all people lived differently. I asked them not to push their concept of normalcy on me. I still stand by this answer and a few friendly outings with Cove will not change it. It'll strengthen it. I'll see for myself the reason why it's better to live in a world where everything—good and bad—happens to everyone but me. That being said, five minutes had passed. It was time to turn off the lights, pet Nabi goodbye and lock the doors. Cove trailed behind me through every step I took and I nearly handed him the keys to lock the door for me since he looked so eager for it to happen.

"Where are we going and what are we doing?" I asked.

"That's pretty direct. You're giving me the impression you want to get it over with." He bit his lip while talking in sarcasm—a language I knew of as much as he did.

"I'm waiting for a direct answer, too."

"You'll never get direct words from me," he said, forgetting an earlier event.

"Didn't you directly say you liked me?"

Him forgetting about it makes it look even more like a joke. My doubts have only gotten stronger.

"About that..." He wriggled his body while speaking. "When it comes to the truth, I have no choice." In a still body, he looked at me with eyes that did not smile.

For a split second, the hair on my arms rose.

"I don't want to put pressure on you. Drop your shoulders and let's go." His eyes creased back to their natural state.

I can't understand this man. To try and dissect his words would be a waste of time I didn't have. I walked to an uncertain destination and didn't even try to guess at this point. It's pointless. A guy this weird could take me places I never knew existed.

"Should I give you a hint?" he said.

"Let's try it out," I said, not believing I could.

He hopped, two feet and hands stuck together while making the noise: "Boing!"

He hopped, he literally hopped. He's no less than a weirdo. What could I understand from this?

"That's your hint?"

"You'll understand it when we arrive."

"What's the point of giving me a hint I won't understand until finding out the answer?"

"It's fun, no?"

No, I wanted to reply.

I already felt it deep in my bones that this outing would be long. A minute felt like an hour, thus an hour would be perceived as a week.

"How far is this place? Do we need to take the bus? I don't have my bus card on me." I did have my bus card but thought I could use this as an excuse to go home, even for a couple of minutes.

"It's at walking distance. It opened only recently, so you might not know about it."

Mr. I came back to town after three years knows of a place I didn't. It's plausible. I require merely a single hand to count the places I know. My exploration is done through books and those places are fictional.

A few more steps on the pavement filled with rocks and we had arrived at a store resembling the witch's house in Hansel and Gretel. The one made of sweets. The roof tiles were coloured in primary colours and resembled candies. I thought it was weird for me to have never noticed it. Perhaps it was overshadowed by all the other coloured roofs in Mardi Town. It is one of the characteristics of this town. We pride ourselves with our unique roofs. It's almost a crime to leave it plain. The walls of the store were gingerbread-coloured, and the door made you want to bite it, as it looked like a solid piece of chocolate.

The sign of the store was decorated with marshmallows and sugar cookies. It read: Bonnie's Bunny Workshop.

"Ta da!" He exclaimed, reaching his arms in direction of the store.

I was even more confused. The hint was clear, but bunny workshop? What could we possibly do there? I followed him in and was immediately welcomed by a scent of ginger, cinnamon and nutmeg.

Sweet and spicy, I thought.

It was my first time here, but I felt at home. The walls, as they were outside, were gingerbread coloured. These ones had texture, a cookie-like texture with grains and lines. I was pleasantly surprised with the amount of bunny dolls stacked on round shelves. Then it clicked. It's a workshop rather than a store who sells bunny dolls. Thus, we'd be here customizing our own bunny dolls. If I smiled right now, I'd give him the wrong idea.

"What do you think?" he asked me, his head tilting to reach the front of mine.

"Let's get it over with."

His lips turned into a line and he brought his head back, nodding.

I would be lying if I said that seeing him so

disappointed didn't hurt. He must have spent quite the time to find this workshop. Honestly, I don't know how he did it. He expected enthusiasm from me and all he got was a cold shoulder. It didn't feel good, but no regret was in my sight. It's better than giving him false hopes; or so I learned from rom-coms. Before the air turned awkward, a woman looking to be in her thirties approached us. Her hair was abnormally black and tied in a low ponytail. She wore a light pink apron embedded with lace on top of a navy blue T-shirt.

"Hello, my dear customers. I'm Bonnie, the owner of this bunny workshop." Her voice, thankfully, hadn't been the obnoxious high-pitched one I'd expected; it was a mature and gentle one. "I assume you're here to make custom bunnies."

"That's right!" said Cove, his voice sounding sugar high.

"If you could take a seat on the biscuit chair, I'll explain to you our process of bunny making."

Making our way to the chairs in biscuit shape, I whispered in Cove's ears: "It's a surprising choice from you. Do you secretly like cute thing?"

"The one I like is cute, so this was an evident choice," he whispered back, making me almost choke on my saliva.

He didn't really answer my question. I wanted to know if he kept cute dolls on his bed and had named each of them. Or if he wore pyjamas with cute characters drawn on them. I wanted to pry, but the owner, Bonnie, started to speak.

"Alright, first, thank you for visiting my small workshop. It will not disappoint you. Here you will craft a new friend, a new companion who will stand by your side no matter what. You can make it in various sizes. Perhaps a small one to use as a key chain or one big enough to hug at night. I'd recommend the regular size, which is neither too big nor too small and can be kept on a shelf and hugged for comfort as well. With this store, I wish to normalize adults carrying a cute plush everywhere."

She spoke with sparks flying in the air, and I enjoyed every word. I too would find it nice to carry around a cute plush. I wondered what Cove thought about it. He blankly stared while she kept on talking.

"To make your bunny is very simple. First,

you choose the skin of the bunny. There are different colours available. Then comes the stuffing. We use a classic fluffy stuffing but you can choose between a couple of objects for added texture such as a mini pearls or newspaper, etc... I offer scent bags you can place into the bunny before closing it. You'll have to stitch the bunny closed yourself; I can teach you basic sewing if ever you need to learn it. Next, in a basket of fabric scraps, you'll choose a small square of your choice to sew on the bunny, wherever you want to place it on. The last step would be clothing. A portion of my store is filled with bunny plush sized clothes. The clothing, fabric, stuffing and scent is included in the price while the clothes are discounted if you are making your first bunny." She let out a long breath, the one she's been holding while giving instructions. "I really need to make info-graphics explaining this process."

"Are you going for the regular size?" he asked me.

"Yes."

"Then I will too."

We went to the corner where on a wooden table laid flat but fluffy bunny skins. I picked a chestnut one while Cove picked the navy coloured one. Having picked all the necessary accessories, we sat down once again.

"Do you know how to sew, Salem?" he asked, looking at the sewing kits, question marks filling his eyes.

"Yes, I guess you don't. Ask for Bonnie's help then."

"No, no. I'd rather learn from you." He moved his chair, inching closer to me. It only made me want to punch him. "So, will you teach me?"

Why do I have the feeling he's lying and he'd keep on doing it. Next, he'd say that he didn't know how to breathe and ask me to teach him.

"I'll fix the thread in your needle first." If I hadn't agreed, he would have persisted and this day truly would have never ended. "While I do that, put in the stuffing."

"I forgot about that part."

How could he? It's the most important one.

For my bunny, aside from the classic stuffing, I put newspaper since I liked the sound it made. Scent-wise, there is only one scent I could not resist: strawberry. I am addicted to strawberries, it's all I think about.

Out of curiosity, I looked over to Cove's side. He added mini seashells to his stuffing. He never breaks character, neither did I. Scent-wise, I sniffed a fresh and slightly briny scent. It was serene to the senses. I asked him about it since the scent bag was already in the bunny.

"The scent of the sea," he answered, a proud tone to him.

I scoffed, finding his consistency as comic as mine.

Now came the sewing part.

"Look at how I do it first. It's very easy. You insert the needle into the fabric and then pull it along with the thread until the knot at the end makes it so you can't pull anymore. You do the same from under."

I showed him the process a couple of times before handing him his threaded needle. He got the hang of it pretty fast. That's it, I'm sure he lied.

"Up and under," he said to himself, as if continuing the act would make me believe it was his first time.

"Tell me, Cove, did you start any of the books?"

I pulled the trigger. Cove's hands froze and his bunny was left half stitched, half opened.

"I did start," he pronounced every letter almost in a melodic way. "I started Peter Pan. I read a chapter; might not be much, but I tried. Focusing was hard."

"It's a common problem. You'll start focusing after a while. The kids at the library are often restless and can never read more than one page. You know what I do then?"

"I am curious and, at the same time, offended because you're about to compare me to kids."

This comment made me laugh because he guessed my exact intention. I didn't try to be discreet about it.

"I read part of the book at loud until it grabs their attention and they reach for the book themselves."

"So you'll read Peter Pan to me?"

"Not a chance. You're not a kid. I can compare you to them, but I won't be using the same method because you seem more hopeless than them. Kids can be annoying, but at least they're cute. You're just annoying."

Hearing this, I thought he'd slam his fists on the table, stand up, throw the bunny away and leave the shop; not wanting to have anything to do with me. Instead, he laughed.

The sound of his bright laughter invaded the shop. It was a sound so clear, it could invite rays of sunshine indoor, without needing a window. And his face; I couldn't help but stare. He looked like the emoji who had carets for eyes. As his head was thrown back, streaks of his blond hair dangled. I don't think I blinked for an entire minute.

"How I love the way you talk, Salem," he said, calming down by taking deep breaths.

Once his eyes regained vision, I turned to focus on the bunny. The faster I sew it up, the faster I can be out of here. In the right ear, I attached a piece of fabric with butterfly motifs and was close to calling it a day. There was one last step. But did a plush really need to wear clothes? I chose the first dress I saw. It was rose gold and had no motifs or words written on it.

"I finished my bunny. Hurry up with yours."

At that time, Bonnie, the bunny doll expert, came to our station. She inspected my bunny and clasped her hands near her cheek.

"My! You did a great job. This bunny is adorable. All that is left is to give it a name."

"A name?"

"Yes, it's your friend."

"I'll have to think about it while my other friend finishes his."

Hearing the word friend, Cove turned his head to me at the speed of lightning.

"That's an improvement. You're calling me your friend."

"Don't misunderstand. It would be too long to explain why we're here, together. A little white lie won't hurt."

With crossed arms, he asked me: "Are you a fridge? Why are you so cold?"

"I'm more of a freezer." I said with a straight face.

Neither I nor he could believe what I just did. It was a joke. I cracked a joke. For the first time in my life, it seems.

"Don't mind me and keep sewing." I said.

"There is no more sewing to do. I'm done with Captain Bunnybeard."

"Captain Bunnybeard? Are you a kid?"

"At heart, yes."

"Fine, I'll think like a kid as well and call mine Strawbunny."

"Oh, how cute!" chimed in Bonnie. "Captain Bunnybeard and Strawbunny. I like how you both used 'bunny' in the names."

It wasn't supposed to go like that. I

shouldn't have been influenced by him to crack a joke and to choose a childish name. Please, let me go so that I can erase today's memories.

"The very last step," she said, the sound of shattered glass filling my head.

What is there left to do?

"There's a rule in my store. If people come make their bunnies together, they must exchange them at the end—making it a meaningful gift to commemorate this activity." Hearing this, I shifted.

"You knew about this, didn't you?"

He feigned ignorance by bringing his shoulders to his ears, but these lips of his could not lie or conceal one.

His lips in his mouth, and he carefully handed me his Captain Bunnybeard. I didn't want to give him Strawbunny. I crafted it with care and in the process imagined what my days would look like with it. Now, I'd spend those days with a bunny who smells like the sea, wears an eye patch and a T-shirt with a skull on it.

"I'm waiting," he said, a whisper to his tone.

I'm waiting as well for this summer to be over and for him to leave town.

Chapter 8

There stared at me Captain Bunnybeard on the shelf of my bedroom. A single black eye, looking at me. I stared at it for so long, it felt like it would bust out a smirk any minute now. Like father, like son. I still can't believe I handed my precious Strawbunny. It's money, time, and energy wasted. How much more will I waste in Cove's company?

Fourteen to go, I repeated in my head, until it begged me to shut up.

"Salem, dinnertime!" I heard my mom shout from downstairs. She'd been waiting to say it. It showed in the bright tone of her voice.

I was rarely in time for our home's dinner time. I ate alone, outside or in my room. This day, because of the outing with Cove, I was back home at an unusual time. And it just happened to be the right time for my parents. Making my way to the dining room, I made eye contact with dad whose smile could not be hidden. It was up to his ears.

"It's been a while since I saw you, Salem. It's weird to say that when we live in the same house."

Both of my parents are the cheerful type and never seem to run out of energy. You would notice I am of a different breed. My energy levels were never high enough to run out, they maintained a similar level— practically one of a monk's. Reading *is* a peaceful activity. I do get frustrated at parts of a book and happier than ever in others but it all happens in my head.

"We all work," I answered him.

"Yes, but you, too much."

My parents think I'm a workaholic because of the amount of time I spend at the library when, in fact, it's the complete opposite. I read more than I work.

"I'm glad you're home," mom said, approaching with a plate of Alfredo pasta in each hand.

My mouth watered at the sight of my favourite meal and my eyes followed it until it rested on my side of the table. My saviour, I called it. The one who brightened this day. I waited with impatience for my parents to take a bite so that I could dig in myself. Rolling the sauce-dipped pasta on my fork, butterflies rose in me.

"Tell me, Salem, why are you here?" My mom always was the talkative type.

All I wanted to do was eat, but here came the questions.

"I had something to do."

"Something other than going to the library?" Her eyes went round and her head to the side.

"Yes."

"Now that's strange," my dad took the relay.

"What's so strange about that?"

I stared at my plate while restricting my left hand from raising the fork to my mouth.

"So where did you go?" asked my mom.

I didn't want to tell them where I went and with whom I went. They'd be more than happy to hear about it, and that is why I'm keeping quiet. I can't handle their enthusiasm and endless questions. To answer the previous question, I'd need a white lie, as they weren't going to change the subject. They know I have no friends, making it impossible for me to say that I was out with a girlfriend. Using Mrs. Elgnis would be risky since she often meets my mom on the way home—her house is in the same direction. The night market wasn't open today and the morning market was…in the morning. Making up a whole other situation would only complicate it, since I'd need to keep on developing the lie and repeat it often. I could one day fall into my own trap by forgetting the minor details I'd made up days or weeks ago. They both looked at me, waiting for an answer that took much too long to be given.

"So, where did you go?"

"I-I stopped by a new shop that lets you customize plush bunnies."

Saying half the truth seemed to be fine. It wouldn't be strange to say I went alone.

"There is? Oh, that sounds cute! You'll have to tell me where it is."

Crap. I'd better inform Bonnie of my lie. If a woman says her daughter came recently and recommended me the place, don't mention the fact I was here with a man, I'd tell her.

"Sure, sure. Now can we eat?"

"Of course. Oh, and don't forget to show me your bunny after dinner. I want to see how much your taste was reflected on it."

Another oh crap incoming. When she sees Captain Bunnybeard, she'll wonder where has her daughter's mind gone to. I shoved my food in, erasing all these nonsensical thoughts.

"This reminds me," *what could a bunny remind her of?* "The son of my friend Isa came back to town after three years. He's here for his summer break."

Why does this ring a bell? Please let it be someone else.

"He went to Mardi High. You might know him."

"Please, our daughter had eyes for the books only. I don't think she even saw her classmates, let alone remember them."

The truth could not offend me.

"It wasn't to that extent. Or was it?" she continued. "Anyway, his name is Cove."

I dropped my fork and almost choked on my mouthful of Alfredo pasta.

"Are you okay?" my dad handed me a glass of water while my mom continued on talking.

"His mom's worried about him. She said he was a bit different. He never talked about his time in college and avoided the subject when asked. She's worried about this summer as well, since none of his friends are here."

Cove didn't seem that different when we talked. But what would I know? I'd need to know how he was like before to notice a change. I only saw him from afar. I'd never spoken to him as much as I have in the past few days.

"I have a favour to ask you, Salem."

Oh, no.

"What do you think of hanging out with him times to times? I know it's not your style to hang out with other people, but it'll be good for you and him. It's not healthy to stay so closed off. And he'll maybe open up to you, seeing that you're of the same age. Sadly, there are things children can't say to their parents because of an age difference."

It's not just the age gap. I can't tell my mom numerous things, such as the fact I am already hanging out with Cove. Admitting it would be embarrassing and refusing it would only make our moms worry.

And since when were our moms friends? How? And why did I just learn of it? So much to think of and so little time.

"Are you going to do it?"

My parents often had to ask me at least

90

twice the same question as I get lost in my world thinking away and fail to notice the time passing.

"I'll think about it."

Isn't this the best answer when wanting to run away from the subject?

"You better think about it," she added, at last planting her fork in the now soggy pasta. I was just about done with mine.

"I'm going back to the library," I said, making my way to the sink.

"It was too good to be true," my mom said, her mouth half full. "Of course, she's going back to the library."

"At least, she ate dinner with us," added dad.

Yes, at least I did. The food was delicious, but the conversation could have been better. Why couldn't she bore us with the usual anthropology stuff? She'd talk of a new discovery or the fascination she has with certain cultures and how this town lacked culture. Mardi Town was perfectly fine, in my opinion. It often was festive and people were of colourful minds. She talked of traditions and clothing. Here, the closest we have to traditional clothing are eye masks from masquerade balls. My mom wants to start new traditions for the town, saying that it doesn't have to be of the past as our current time will someday become a far-away past. In her free time, she draws out sketches of traditional clothing and, like a novelist, creates some legends that are modern yet still as strange.

"Don't be too late," she says, repeating that line every night.

"I won't," I said, not knowing if I meant it or not. Losing track of time is what I do.

Going back to the library even if I am dead tired is a must. I promised Nabi. I know that she's a cat who doesn't understand the concept of a promise. But I also know that Nabi is still a kitty. She came to us, merely days, or perhaps a month to her. Back then, I could not let that poor kitten sleep alone in the library and sneaked out of the house and slept by her side. I'd come back home early enough for my parents to suspect nothing. The more she grew, the less I'd needed to keep her company at night. Nabi neared the event where she'd become an adult cat. They say that at one-year-old, a kitten turns into cat. For me, she'll forever remain a baby. I still need to check up on her before bedtime.

Walking in the streets that lacked the presence of the sun, I thought of the other night and hoped the past wouldn't repeat itself. If Cove was in front of the library, again, I'd dash to enter from the back. I'm not letting him in again. He'll have to wait for the morning to come like the others. It was a onetime-thing. A not-to-be repeated thing. That is, if he is standing, waiting for me like a fool with no confirmation that I'd be coming.

As I hoped, the only one who waited for me tonight was sweet little Nabi. She might not be so little anymore. That made me more sad than it should have. Time flies by without any notice, not that I would have noticed the notice. My world doesn't comprehend the concept of time. I get shocked now and then when I put my head out to the real world. It's like an astronaut coming back from space to find that years had passed and people aged. These days, I find myself out of my cocoon more than I desired to. It leads me to think that time waits for none.

Chapter 9

"Are you ready for our next date?" he said, holding on to the straps of his backpack that had the colour of a stormy sky.

Is it just me or that bag looks too small, making it tight around the shoulders? Maybe he had something heavy in there because the bag seemed to pull him back a bit. His feet were especially stuck to the pavement.

"Friendly outing," I reminded him.

He looked away, pretending he hadn't heard.

"Are you taking good care of Captain Bunnybeard?" he asked, out of the blue or to change the subject.

"He's on the shelf."

"The shelf? You're letting the poor captain on a shelf?" His lower lip slid out and he continued, "Me, I slept hugging Strawbunny. Don't you smell the strawberry on me?"

I was disgusted and terrified. If I did the same, I'd be smelling like the sea. I took a couple of steps towards him to see if he'd really have a strawberry scent on him. It was faint, but it confirmed his statement.

"I suppose, but—"

He came even closer than I did, his nose millimetres away from my neck. I held my breath and froze on the spot. There I could feel the smile on his face without having to see it. I felt the corners of his lips rising with the sound of his breath and the nearness of his lips and chin. Why would he check my neck? The bunny isn't bottled perfume. Even if I hugged it, the scent wouldn't be on my neck. Or would it? The last time I hugged a plush to sleep was in elementary school.

"You smell just like me, strawberry," he said, pulling back.

"It's my perfume," I said, avoiding eye contact.

"I'm happy to now have something in common with you."

"Let's make this outing fast and short," I said, walking ahead, not knowing where to go.

"It's that side," he said, pointing to the opposite side.

Walking to the right side, I made sure there was more than enough space between us, as in the space for a truck to pass by and its wind to not even graze us. In contrary to my intentions, with each step, the distance shortened. Turns out he copied the pace of my feet and followed them wherever.

"I don't have a hint this time?" I asked.

"Would you like a hint?"

"I wouldn't be asking if I didn't."

It was embarrassing enough to ask once. Did he really have to make me ask twice?

"Alright. Today's hint is..." He took a big bite of the air, shutting his eyes tight.

Another shock to my brain and my eyes.

'The heck is wrong with you?' I wanted to ask, but that would be showing interest.

"This hint, you'll understand it once we get there as well."

I'd rather not.

In fact, we'd arrived to our destination,

and that hint was still in the air with his imaginary bite. We were at the park where the grass was abnormally green and the benches were burning hot.

"Follow me," he said, as if the park was big enough for him to have a favourite spot when, in reality, there were only two benches separated by the actual space a truck would need to pass. Cove hadn't wandered to a bench. No, he brought me to the centre of the park, where stood the field of grass and nothing else other than wild flowers. Let's hope he has a mat or a towel in this heavy bag of his. I wore beige wide-legged pants. If they turn green, I'll rip up Captain Bunnybeard in front of him.

"You can sit down, you know."

While I lost myself in a monologue, he'd already sat down on the bare grass. I dipped my hand first to see if it was wet. Lucky for me, it was dry and even crispy to the ear. I guessed it wouldn't hurt to sit down and watched while he put his hand in the backpack—the one that was about to fall off or make him fall. He grunted when taking out the mystery object, which I presume is the main character of this outing and screamed:

"Ta-da!"

A watermelon. This man had a whole watermelon on his back. Also, this was the main event. I don't know which part I should be more surprised by. I'd previously spent days worrying about this outing. Every day, the nerves ate me up alive. I'd fear the eye contacts. When he'd tell me 'good morning', I'd fear he'd add we have a date tonight. If we'd exchange custom bunnies on the first, at this pace, I thought we'd exchange rings on the second. But, no, we're eating a watermelon. How would we even cut it out here?

"Surprised by the simplicity, aren't you? That's what summer is all about!" He said, his eyes moving towards the sky, which had little to no clouds.

A bright summer day it is.

"Do you really want to use your friendly outing opportunity on a watermelon?" I asked, to be sure.

I shouldn't have asked really, since it benefited me to have it so easy. My mission was to eat watermelon; it couldn't get better than this. No, with Cove, it could only get harder.

"It's an investment," he said, his eyes sparkling.

His legs were crossed and, for the most part, bare. He wore his beige cargo shorts today, and they lifted a bit higher when he sat. He, unlike me, wasn't afraid to stain his beige-coloured bottoms. On top, he wore a sweatshirt matching the colour of the watermelon. This colour went well with his blond hair. No, I'd better retract my words. Can I?

Anyhow, he placed the watermelon in front and stared at it with deep concentration, as if he were to open it using his mind.

"How did you think you were going to open it?"

He gave me the most mischievous smile I'd seen, "With my head."

My eyes popped off. "You can't be serious."

"What am I if not serious?"

I don't think he'd want to hear my

response to that. The list is surprisingly long.

"I don't want this outing to end at the hospital. Don't do it."

"I won't hurt my head. It's a nutcase."

At least he knows.

He placed each of his hand on the side of the fruit and furrowed his eyebrows while continuously piercing the fruit with his eyes. Cove was ready to throw his head until I stopped him halfway by placing my hand on his forehead. I should have taken the fruit away and let him bang his head on the grass. It would have been painful but not deadly. I lifted back his head.

"You're worried about me," he said, taking a hold of my wrist before I could remove it.

"I'm worried about the watermelon. I don't want to taste the iron of your blood in it. That'll ruin the taste and the only good part of this outing."

He let go of my wrist, a smile on his face. It seems my words were not convincing enough.

"In all seriousness, we really need to cut this fruit."

"You didn't bring a knife or something

similar?"

It took him days to ask me out on this second outing and all he'd prepare was a fruit without the bare minimum, a tool to open it. He must be quite aware of his identity, a tool, so much that he only brought himself.

"If I can't with my head, I'll try with my hand."

The ideas that came out of his head were...special. The worst part was that he was dead serious. People could say they'll cut open a watermelon with their hands, but that would be for laughs. They'd never attempt it. Cove prepared a fist and this time, I didn't have the time to stop him. He threw it and in the span of a single second; he broke the fruit in half. It was a clean cut that made little to no sound. My mouth wide opened, I went back and forth from the watermelon and Cove who winced, holding his fist now redder than what he'd split. The urge to hold his hand was heavy.

"Why are you this stupid?" I told him.

He laughed through the pain and looked at me with a radiant smile, his set of teeth out for the world to see, in this case, only for me.

"We can eat," he said, taking out two spoons from his bag. And at this point, I didn't care to know if they were clean or not. He nearly broke his hand for us to eat. On second thoughts, he may have broken his hand. Only time will tell. Or if his hand turns purple, then we'll know for sure.

"Are you sure you can eat?"

"Will you feed me if I say that I can't?" He held his hand and threw himself to the floor, whining like a baby.

I felt bad at him first when I saw the redness, but all emotion flew with the passing breeze. Now, he was exaggerating.

"Your other hand is perfectly fine."

"After all I did for you, you're still cold. I could even call you cruel." He sat back up, scooping out the fruit with his left hand. He struggled a while, but eventually got the hang of it.

I hate when people say 'after all I did for you'. I asked nothing of you. A good act, a selfless act, is to do without expecting something in return. These words that make them look like victims are a mask no one's been brave enough to call hypocrite.

I tasted the fruit myself scooping out from the enormous half. Thank the stars, it was sweet. I wouldn't have forgiven him if he'd picked one that tasted like cucumbers.

"What a beautiful day," he said.

It would have been if he hadn't announced it. Words that come from that mouth started to lose meaning to me.

"I don't think we can finish a whole watermelon by ourselves," I remarked, stabbing the fruit with my spoon.

"Trust me, we can. It's mostly water and we'll lose track of time speaking and eating. It's like popcorn when watching a movie. You could unconsciously eat the entire bag and wonder who ate it at the end of the movie."

"And you think we'll talk?"

"You don't have to. I'll do all the talking and you listen," he said, a more gentle tone to him. "You're wearing a cute shirt today. It says: dreams are made of sun, sand and coconut. It's not wrong."

"The lines on my clothes are never

wrong."

"What about mine?" he asked, pointing to a fine print on the bottom of his sweatshirt.

"Utopia is near," I read. "What is your Utopia?" I asked him, knowing that this concept is more so an opinion different for everyone.

"My Utopia, huh?" He stared off at the sky again in deep thoughts.

It was indeed something to think about. I thought of it as well, knowing he'd bounce the question back to me after.

"I don't see it as good," he began, intriguing layers in my mind. "Perfection is risky. Being excessively perfect seems fishy. I think Utopia would be a counterfeit. Smiles wouldn't really be smiles but they wouldn't hide anything either. A world controlled by a sole emotion—happiness—doesn't look as appealing to me." He hadn't taken his eyes off the sky while speaking as if the words were being displayed there.

Looking at the sky myself, a sudden thought came over to me.

"Did you know that the sky we see is not really blue?"

"What is it then?"

"It's violet. We discern it as blue because of the sensitivity of our retina. It's a shame, really. I wish I could see this violet sky."

"Hearing about it makes me want to see it as well. Now, what about your Utopia?"

I'd spoken about something else, hoping we'd skip my answer. What more could I say after hearing such an opinion? It was similar to mine, and that was a shocker. I refused to admit we had something in common, especially with a guy who doesn't read. Arriving at a dead end, I could only explain my Utopia. However, I changed my answer to bring some positivity.

"The land of youth. The land where I'd run in a field of grass. The land I'd wander to after a long journey. The answer to all the questions I've asked the universe. A place that feels like home. The light I'd been chasing. The place I saw in a dream that was bittersweet."

The sky was strange today. It both made us say things out of character.

"I see," he calmly said. "You could also see it this way."

His view was more towards a dystopian system where the government would decide what was good for us and what wasn't, while my view was a sentimental one—the yearning for a place that probably doesn't exist.

"So, Cove, did you get to read a bit more?" I asked, and that's what it took to get the sky out of his vision and a huge chunk of fruit in his mouth.

"I- can't- speak- with my mouth full."

Chapter 10

"Perhaps even with the dream of wonderland of long ago: and how she would feel with all their simple sorrows, and find a pleasure in all their simple joys, remembering her own child-life, and the happy summer days. The end."

It took weeks to finish the tale of Alice's Adventure In Wonderland. This story wasn't exactly one I could read in a single sitting. Once a week, a couple of elementary students sat on the round rainbow-coloured carpet to hear a tale. Each librarian has the task of finding a tale and study it to be able to answer the question of the curious little children.

"Ms. Salem, does Wonderland exist?"

I asked them to call me by my first name since it'd be awkward for my last name to be used by kids when I myself was still young.

"Yes. Where could we find it?" another asked.

"At night, when you close your eyes and fall into a deep sleep, you might have the chance to see Wonderland for yourself."

I didn't need a white lie for this one since even in the story, Wonderland was, in reality, a dream.

"Why would you want to go to Wonderland? It's a scary place," remarked a girl. "I don't want to get big or tiny or get my head cut off."

I was starting to think this story was a tad bit violent for children. I can't even count how much the word 'behead' was mentioned. A boy wearing a yellow t-shirt stood up with fists tightened. "I want to get big and stomp around the town to fight dragons."

"Dragons don't exist..." another whispered from behind.

"Me, I want to be tiny and live in my dollhouse," said the little girl wearing a cute summer dress.

"Me, I want to be the queen and I'll behead all of you," said another girl, standing up.

That's when the chaos started. I shouldn't have taught them this word. They wouldn't have needed this word in the future anyway. Some things were better hidden, alas, it's too late. They ran after each other, pretending to be characters from Alice In Wonderland. One held their hands to the air, adding to their height for the role of a giant. One brought their whole body forth, trying to seem tinier than they already were. Another hopped as Cove had done a couple of days ago, pretending to be a bunny. The funniest was the girl who proclaimed herself as queen of hearts; she did the chasing.

"Whoa, whoa kids, remember, this is a library. What do you do in a library? You stay quiet. If you want to play, you can go outside, behind the library."

Without even answering, they ran—continuing their game—to the back door.

"They're very noisy today. It must have been a fun story," said Ms. Elgnis, from behind.

"Alice In Wonderland. I think I made the wrong choice." Placing a hand over my forehead.

"Why? It's a classic."

"Because of me, they're talking about beheading each other. I should've read a censored version."

There's something about classic tales for children. The original version always comes with a language vastly different from our times. That is why there are adaptations. But I preferred the rawness of the original. I also feel that I am respecting the author by reading it this way.

Ms. Elgnis laughed hysterically. "They're children. They don't mean what they say."

"I do hope you're right."

I didn't want to see angry parents in front of my station telling me how irresponsible it was of me to teach such a language to their children. Or worst, to hear on the news that a child beheaded another. The pessimist in me occasionally makes its appearance to remind me of its existence. I couldn't help but to bite my nails and keep checking the window. If I saw anything close to a beheading in the garden, I'd rush out.

Ms. Elgnis brought back my attention with a tap on the shoulder. "I can't wait for the annual Glass Wing picnic," she said, taking small leaps in the same place. The curly bob of hair on her head bounced with every leap. "How are the preparations going?"

Each year, Ms. Elgnis planned the event,

and I was a volunteer. This year, I am the one organizing it. Indirectly, it's a test for me—to see if I am fit for the job of librarian as this is an important tradition for Glass Wing. They wish to continue this event for eternity, literally. As I am young, I'll probably stay here for a very long time and one day end up training the ones who'll keep the event alive, as Mrs. Elgnis did with me. I learned from the previous years and now, Mrs. Elgnis has completely taken her hands off. She's neither allowed to help me or critique anything. She is a bystander.

"Everything is going as planned," it always had been.

I've attended events organized by the library since I was a little girl and dreamed of making one as well. I've filled notebooks with ideas for picnics, author events, reading events, etc... I have binders filled with pictures I'd taken from the events and reference pictures cut out from magazines. I've been waiting for this control.

"I'm sure you do have everything planned. I know I can trust you."

"Yes, you can," I told her, feeling the warmth behind her words.

She was the epitome of a lady librarian and close to a mother figure to me. It would be better to say that she's like my aunt from another grandmother. Ms. Elgnis left to the garden where the children played with a smile on. With her there, I could take my eyes off. There will be no beheading in her presence.

"Did I hear something about a picnic?" Cove said coming from—I don't know where he came from.

Not even his shadow had warned me of his presence. There was no sign of him in the library earlier, and that was strange. Was he hiding from me all this time? To overhear my conversations? The storytelling? Now that is stalker behaviour.

"I've been meaning to ask you. What does Glass Wing mean? And why is the library named Glass Wing?"

"If you'd read the plaque at the entrance, you'd know. Glass Wing is a rare type of butterfly whose wings resemble glass because of their transparency. And years and years ago on the opening day of the library, a Glass Wing butterfly was seen by the director. Since he was unsatisfied by the name of the library—it was supposed to be called the Mardi Town library—he saw the appearance of this butterfly as a sign and quite literally changed the sign at the front with the name Glass Wing."

"Oh wow. As much as I like this story, I have a feeling you could have told it better, just like you did for Alice's adventures in Wonderland."

That's it. He's been here for a while. And of course, I'd want to tell this story with enthusiasm. It's a beautiful story about a butterfly, my favourite. Seeing Cove, I couldn't bring up the emotions. I just couldn't.

"And about that picnic..." he continued, and I didn't like where it was going. "You're already so busy with your work, it seems hard to take on an entire event by yourself-"

"I'm perfectly capable of doing it by myself."

"I could help!"

"No, you can't."

"I could!"

"Never."

"Do not attempt too much at once, the boy and the filberts," he said, his chin raised.

I see he's read a bit of Aesop's fables. To remember the exact words and title, he must have a photographic memory. As impressed as

I was, there was no convincing done. We were already spending so much time together with these silly outings. And he came daily to the library to start nonsensical conversations. Working on the picnic together would make us spend nearly the twenty-four hours a day has to offer.

"Every man should be content to mind his own business, the seagull and the kite." I knew my fables as well.

"In unity, there's strength, the lion and the three bulls," he said, speedily bragging of his memory and using my challenge against me.

"Evil companions bring more hurt than profit, the sick stag."

"But I'm not evil."

"You can't control how you look to others. I decide if you're evil or not, in my eyes."

"Would someone evil bring you out to eat a watermelon and make custom bunnies? And would someone evil bring you to the hottest place in town tomorrow?"

"The devil could walk me to the park if he wanted to."

I didn't even want to know what this *'hottest place'* he talked about was. In my head, I counted off the outings, one by one. If we take away tomorrow's, there were twelve left.

The number was a long wall I'd need to break down and use as a bridge to cross back to my own little world.

"Why would the devil walk you to the park?" he asked, raising an eyebrow.

"Because I'm pretty," I said, running away to hide between shelves.

With that line, surely he'll leave me alone. Spoiler alert, he didn't. He came running after me, grinning like the joker.

"At least you know."

With that, I cringed and covered my face with all the books I could hold.

"Let me help you with the Glass Wing picnic, pretty Salem." He said, attempting to remove the books from my face.

"No way!" I fought off his hands and held on to these books for dear life.

I hid my face because it was strawberry red. I could feel my cheeks burning. Revealing it would only complicate the matter that is this summer break.

"Don't you want to lead a meeting by explaining the plan and hand out the tasks?"

His words went right through my heart. He understood my personality impeccably. I was tempted to take him up on his offer. In this library, I was the youngest and wouldn't get the opportunity to lead a meeting until I'd grown older and there were younger people working by my side. I worried this day would almost never come, as this was a library. Even now, the only librarians were Ms. Elgnis and I; we have weekend staffs but they are often changed. Our director, Mrs. Revef, is away most of the time, having not much work to do. Nowadays, she came in solely for papers that were required to be signed by the highest authority of the library. One day, I'll be that highest authority. Look out, Mrs. Revef; I am always running towards that seat. All that to say that I wasn't about to lose more of my alone time.

"My answer stands."

"And my offer stands," he says, taking the books out of my hands and on to the shelves.

His hands brushed my hands ever so slightly and I must have mistaken this feeling in me. Surely they were not butterflies, but bees buzzing away. The world around me turned to slow motion while he looked me right in the eyes. And it wasn't bells I heard, but a drumming sound. His chest faced me, who gave my back to the shelf. I couldn't help it; I was mesmerized by a beauty only I could see. Of course, Cove was always a very handsome man and everyone thought so. Seeing him up close was different. You could see every little detail and every poisonous thoughts you had were reflected on his face. I couldn't help to think of the olden days where it was I who looked for him. Now, it being the contrary is nothing else but odd. Cove, what have you done to me? Why are you doing this to me when I'll be left alone at the end of the summer, yet again.

Chapter 11

4:00 am

You've seen the time right. It is currently four in the morning and I am shivering in the dark, the Glass Wing library behind me. This was our meeting point. This '*hottest*' place turned out to truly be a '*hot*' place, and you'd need to be in line early on to have a chance. I've lived here longer, but he already knew the new places that opened in the last three years.

"Boo!" I heard from behind me, feeling two hands on my shoulders.

I'd prepared myself for his surprise attack. It was such a Cove thing to do.

"Did you think I'd scream and jump in your arms?" I told him, a look of pure disgust on my face.

Though I was expecting it, my heart

jumped out of my chest and all I wanted to do was beat him up. Sadly, many laws prevented me from doing so. I'd have to content myself with imagining such a scene.

"Good morning, pretty Salem." He'd given me a nickname based on something I said myself. Only I could dig my own grave.

"I should be inside a dream at this time, but here I am, awake." My eyes could barely hold the weight of my eyelids.

Ever since that alarm rang at a time where the sky was still dark, I woke from the wrong side of the bed and my biological clock was ruined.

"To make you feel better, I'll make this outing feel like a dream."

"No need, it's already a nightmare."

"Now, now, pretty Salem, don't be so harsh."

I'd strangled him in my mind, his neck redder than his shorts that could be seen from far away, like traffic lights. Weren't his legs cold? The summer had only started and at this witching hour; the breeze was at its coldest. At least he wore a hoodie, navy blue just like his child Captain Bunnybeard, with a rather nice sentence written on: For us who are made of stars.

"Are you staring at my pretty legs or are you worried about me?" he said, blinking his eyes.

"I was looking at the ground and that certain spot happened to be next to your legs." I said, shifting my eyes to the floor.

"What spot?" he said, lowering his head to look for a spot we both knew didn't exist. There wasn't anything special about this floor.

"Why did you wear shorts?" I mustered the courage and blurted out what troubled my mind.

"I feel good in those shorts, whether it's cold or hot."

Those running shorts were his natural habitat. No wonder he feels comfortable.

"We should get going," he said, walking ahead. "If we go any later, we won't get a chance to try them."

"What is 'them' you are talking of?"

"You'll see."

"No hint this time around?"

"Baffled."

"And I'll understand the hint once we arrive, right?"

"You're getting the hang of it, pretty Salem."

"If you'd stop calling me pretty Salem, I'd highly appreciate it."

"Is it wrong to call something pretty if I think it?"

"Something? I'm a thing now?"

"No, you're a precious human being. It's just a way of talking."

Not me thinking I could get used to this voice. It was no use. This voice would leave as well before the leaves fell and the trees lost their volume. I let him ramble on, having no energy to do so myself.

"You have no right to stop me from calling you pretty, pretty Salem. I decide for myself, being an adult."

He sure wasn't acting like one.

"Don't take this pleasure away from me."

The word pleasure almost brought back up last night's dinner.

"You took away from me more than I refused you," I replied.

"And what did I take away from you?" he asked, his hands placed on his waist.

"My time, my sleep, my freedom."

"Freedom is a bold word to use."

"I like to use bold words while you should refrain from using them."

"I've noticed sometimes, Salem, you talk like a book."

I saw it as a compliment and this was the kind I liked.

"Thank you."

"I'm glad you didn't misunderstand this one."

This line made me happier since I took it the way it was meant to be taken. Normally, if others told me I talked like a book, they would mean it in a stuffy way. Cove meant it as a positive point.

***

The sun had yet to rise and yet a couple of people already stood in line for a closed stand providing the only light around here with a large neon sign reading: Baffled by a Waffle. I got the hint and immediately wanted to jump back in my bed because I didn't just wake up at 3:30 in the morning to be in front of the library by four for waffles that I have in my freezer. I looked at Cove, the desire to end him rising faster than the sun.

"Waffles?"

"I'm sure you are baffled, but it's worth it,

or so I've heard."

For the first time, he did his best to avoid my eyes. Sadly, there was no turning back as others joined us in line and we were in the middle. I was surprised there was a line at this time of the day in Mardi Town. Never have I seen that in my life. And never would I have expected it.

"They better be worth it," I said, surrendering to the situation.

I should have added conditions to our challenge, such as no outings during early and or late hours.

"They're the best in town. If you don't believe me, check the reviews. Plus, they only sell a hundred a day. After that, they close the stand and open twice a week. Rather than despising me, you'll be grateful that I made you come at the right time. You'll see, it's gonna get crowded soon." Cove spoke as if he secretly worked for them. Maybe he was part of their marketing team, and this *friendly outing'* proposition was a ruse to get me to eat waffles. If only it had been his plan. The waffles would have been the end of it. Seeing the number of *friendly outings'* we have left, the waffles are only the tip of the iceberg.

"When do they open?" I asked him.

"9 am."

"What?"

He'd mutter the number nine like it was only an hour away. It wasn't.

"You're telling me we have to wait in line for hours?"

I was ready to give up the challenge, take back the reading list, and let him trail behind me like a dog for the rest of the summer. The motifs on my imaginary leash had already been chosen.

"Don't worry," he said, waving his hands. "I prepared everything from camping chairs to snacks."

"If we eat snacks, we won't have an appetite for waffles," I remarked.

"True, we'll have to content ourselves with games. What do you want to do, cards, building blocks?"

"Building blocks? In the middle of the streets?"

"I brought a portable table."

Dumbfounded is an understatement for my feelings.

"Let's sit down," he continued, taking out his folding chairs, a red one and a green one.

He patted down every wrinkle before offering me a seat. Doing so showed some remorse of his part. This outing was going too far and I couldn't hide this emotion. Everything on my face was tight, from my forehead to my lips pressed together.

"You could have waited here, alone, and called me when the waffle stand opened."

"No, no," he said, waving a finger in front of me. "You'd miss out on all the fun. This is the crucial part of the outing."

He talked like he knew of this kind of fun. As if he had memories of standing in line with friends, laughing and being silly. Would he have the same amount of fun with me? I'm not a fun person nor was I a good friend—not having experienced being one at all. Everything I did with Cove was new to me and, to be honest, I don't know how to handle it. Though I didn't care for Cove, part of me didn't want to disappoint him; as I would for a stranger. The desire to please people is human instincts. Sometimes, it's as if eyes observed my every move. I was conscious of the air. I thought that if I tripped, someone would laugh. If my hair was a mess, people would be embarrassed for me. If I walked in a straight posture with a smile on my face, then I'd be the perfect example. Instinctively, these stupid thoughts crossed my mind daily. I wonder how a bright and confident person like Cove would think when walking the streets. Maybe he'd have the leisure of enjoying the weather.

"Where is your head at?" asked Cove, tilting his head towards mine.

I guess I must have been out of it for a while, lost in my stupid thoughts.

"Nowhere."

"Mine, also," he said, striking a nerve of curiosity.

I wanted to ask him to elaborate and continue the subject, but it was tricky.

Mustering the courage, I changed up the question and threw it, "Usually, where is your mind at?"

"It's lost in the middle of nowhere."

What more could I say when he's not explaining?

We could go with: "How is life out of Mardi Town? You never talked about it?"

This must have been a trigger for him as he let out a long sigh, his hands pressed against his legs.

"It's... an experience."

Were his words always this short?

If that time had been enjoyable, I'm sure he'd talk endlessly about it. Seeing it's not the case and seeing that his sunshine dims when the subject comes, it must not have been great.

After a long pause, he spoke, "It wasn't what I excepted, not that I expected much to begin with."

"Out of your low expectations, which ones were broken?"

"I had only one. I thought I'd be okay. I thought I'd come to terms with growing up and becoming a serious adult. My inner child didn't seem to agree with my intentions and I never truly became an adult. I'm the Peter Pan of Mardi Town, aren't I?"

"You don't want to be Peter Pan, trust me. He has an unpleasant personality."

"Having read a bit of it, I get what you're saying."

"What is an adult for you?" I asked, my soul inching closer to his.

Straightening his back, he began to give me a description of the serious adult in his mind. "Someone mature who has their life under control, has a path traced out in front of them, has their future planned and their retirement funds started. Someone who knows their priorities and never wanders off the road."

You have it all wrong, Cove. So much that I don't know where to begin.

"The word adult is just a term. You don't become someone new when growing up. You stay yourself till the end. Don't burden yourself with standards that don't apply to everyone. Off-road is, for some, the best road."

Cove looked at me as if I'd opened mystical doors and brought light the sun hadn't given us, yet. Tugging on the armrest of my chair, he approached, making our noses nearly touch.

"I always knew you could speak so well. I knew if I was patient enough, I'd get some advice out of you."

"Was this all on purpose, then?" I said, doubting his previous words. Was sympathy their purpose?

"Never."

Why was his nose still in front of mine? And why did he pierce my eyes with his? I pushed his shoulder away using minimal force.

"Then what is your purpose?" I threw at him this question, not knowing what I would answer if it was given to me.

"I don't have one. I don't even know the

meaning of it. I thought I could live without one, following the outline printed on the tracks."

He didn't look at me anymore. His eyes were on the floor where stood the invisible printed lines he talked about, blond strands of hair hiding his eyes.

"A purpose can be your passion or simply the person you'd want to become."

I wanted to remove the curtain, put the strands behind his ears, and observe his expression. I could only see the corners of his lips dropping. I couldn't reach my hand and left it up to the wind or his mood swings. The mood swing had been first as he lifted his head, a smile decorating his face. His hair had naturally left the proximity of his face.

"I see," he said. "My passion? The type of person I'd like to become? Even when hearing the description, I don't have an answer. Your passion must be working in the library, then."

"When you hear the word passion, you wouldn't think of the mundane life of a librarian. Rather than saying it's my passion, I'd say it's my safe place. I get to be surrounded by the books I love."

"So, it's not your passion?" he tilted his

head in confusion.

"It's my dream job, but I don't consider it my passion."

"You lost me here," he said, adjusting his body on the chair.

"A passion doesn't necessarily have to be a job. For you, I think it is"

"What do you know that I don't? It's suspicious. Can you see the future? If so, do tell me what it'll look like for me."

I don't see the future Cove. Like you, I remember the past and that's enough to know of your future.

"I've seen your passion years ago. I saw the fire in your eyes and the desire to push your limits. It was the first and last time I'd seen it from someone." I told him.

When he ran on the tracks, Cove was in his own world. He was his own rival and motivation. Seeing that there must have been a painful reason for him to give up running—the love of his life—I was afraid to mention it. Instead, I was brief, hoping he'd bring it up himself.

Why did you run away, Cove?

Chapter 12

Cove's point of view

Her revelation was as shocking as it was confusing. How could she know something about me I didn't? Was it written on my forehead? Is that why I couldn't see it?

"What do you know?" I asked her again.

"I know because I..." Salem trailed her words in order to lengthen a sentence she couldn't finish.

"You have to help me here, pretty Salem."

Whoops, I dug my grave. I made her switch the subject by provoking her with the nickname she hates—but I love. It rolls off the tongue so easily with a hint of sweetness lingering for a while. Giving is as rewarding as receiving.

"Stop calling me that," she said, swinging

my bag at me.

I laughed while being hit. That was a first. Was she turning me into a masochist? The pain from a bag with boxes of building blocks was dopamine, and it felt like we were two characters in a high school melodrama. At that moment, my only wish was for the sun to never rise and the clock to never strike nine. Is it too much to ask for?

Satisfied with the amount of times she hit me, at last, she settled back down on her chair.

"Remind yourself of this moment. If you call me that again, you know what awaits you."

"You really talk like a book; it's like we're inside a fantasy novel and you've just threatened a whole line of my family." I said, earning a humble yet amused smile from her.

"When did I threaten a whole line of your family? I don't take it out on innocents. You're the only sinner I have my eyes on."

"You have your eyes on me?"

"Only for all the wrong reasons."

"That's enough for me."

Silence filled our bubble for the right reasons.

I tried to initiate a staring contest, but she pointed her eyes elsewhere. In front of me was the Salem I knew back in high school, the shy girl. Over the years, yes, she's gotten more confident, and that was a good look on her. But now and then, I got to have glimpses of the cute girl that caught my eye back then. Cute rosy cheeks and eyes with evasive tendencies.

"Wake me up when it's open," she told me, closing her eyes and leaning on the chair.

She evaded in various ways.

"It's mean to leave me awake by myself in this line," I said, forcing a pout out of me.

"It's mean to bring me somewhere I'd need to wait hours for without prior notice."

"Would it have changed a thing if I'd told you?"

"I would have prepared things to do. I would have brought books with me."

"Don't you always have a book on you?"

"Not today. I was afraid of where we'd go and decided to not take one in case it got damaged."

"Where did you think I'd bring you? An underground ring? For a book to be damaged, you'd need to fight and use the book as a shield."

"I'd never bring a book to a fight. I'd rather use my arms as a shield."

"And I'd never bring you to a fight. Now, what do you say we start building? I have a bookstore set for you."

Taking out the box, I waved it in front of her. Seeing the picture of a miniature bookstore, her shy eyes rounded and grew large.

"It can't be helped, I suppose," she answered, bliss hidden in that monotone line.

Eager to start, I set the folding table and the building blocks sets. To share this hobby of mine with none other than Salem made me the happiest I've been in a while.

"Your bag sure is bigger than it looks. It must have been painful to walk around carrying such unconventional items. I'm afraid you'll one day try to bring a whole refrigerator in it, Cove."

"It might not fit my bag, but I could pull it on a dolly cart."

"That's what makes you a weird person, Cove. Normal people would laugh it off, say that even for them, it's impossible and end it here."

We continued to bicker while taking out the manuals for our building blocks. These kinds of arguments at dawn is my cup of tea. It was so sweet it didn't require sugar cubes.

"As a longtime block builder, I have some advice."

"I'm not five and you surely aren't as good as you say you are." Pushing the packets, she continued, "Here's your side of the table and here's mine. You do you and I do me, capiche?"

"Why not hear my advice too? It's your choice to follow or not to."

"Talk then. I won't be looking at you while you talk. I'll be busy building away."

"As you please."

"You're the one who's talking like a book now."

Maybe I did start talking like a book. Having read some fables and a couple of chapters of Peter Pan influenced me. On second thoughts, Salem's company was a more powerful influence.

"Hmm, begin by the bag number one, open only that one to not get it mixed up with the rest. The instructions on the manual are separated by bags, so read the manual category by category."

"That's your advice? Like I said, I'm not five and your advice shows how banal your level is. This may be the only thing normal about you."

"The table's not too spacious, so careful to not drop them. they'll be taken away by the ants."

"Ants? You should've said the wind, it's more realistic. Ants don't have the strength for blocks."

"If they carry it together, they sure can. In unity, there's strength, three bullocks and a lion."

"In this story, the bullocks had to stay together in order to not be eaten by the lion. It's different from ants working together to move a block."

"But we can use this saying in all sorts of discussions."

"I don't know why we're still discussing ants and fables. Let's stay quiet for a while and focus on building our sets."

And so we did. We both shut our mouths and built away. I am a bit disappointed that she didn't ask me what I was building. Was Salem uniquely a distant person or did she have zero interest in me? I didn't mind it at first, thinking that we'd grow closer within the first couple of outings. Sadly, I feel as if she is pushing me away each time. Not knowing the reason behind each push is frustrating. Will I be able to get to that heart of hers? The road there sure is tough.

***

ASMR-like sounds of blocks connecting with each other blended with the sounds of nature waking up. Morning birds chirped away from farther than the human eye could perceive. The wind blew on many things; leaves, plastic bags thrown on the roads, the sleeves of her khaki blouse. The sky had turned a shade brighter, acting as a countdown, reminding me of our time limit. And the line behind us had doubled in size. Salem had eyes for the blocks only and had almost finished her bookshop. I, the expert, was behind. You could guess why.

"You're going to make a hole on my face if you keep staring," she said, startling me.

I suppose you could feel it if someone was staring at you; by the extensive field of vision your eyes have to offer or by instinct alone. You sure could.

"I shouldn't make a hole on that pretty face," I replied, looking away, to the pile of blocks yet to be used.

"I shouldn't have said a word."

"You said a word; now I beg of you to say a couple more. I can't stand this silence." I rubbed the palm of my hands, showing the sincerity of my request.

"Did you get to read?"

This time it was I who shouldn't have said a word.

"I'm halfway Peter Pan."

"You have to read the hidden time next and with your reading speed, I recommend you start even today."

"What's the hurry? I have all summer and why the hidden time precisely? Is it the best book? If it is, haven't you heard of save the best for last?"

"The reason behind this recommendation is Glass Wing personal only information."

I let out a laugh and ended on a grin. If only she knew. Well, I could show her. From the pocket of my shorts, I took out a badge and shoved it right in her range of view—the nearly completed roof of the bookshop.

"I am personnel."

"What's this?" she asked, taking a hold of the badge.

A paper card showing the words 'Volunteer at Glass Wing' was slipped in a plastic pocket attached to a long fabric necklace. Salem had kept a poker face on, but her hands that crippled the ends of the badge could not lie.

"Did you steal it or make it yourself?"

"Nope, I asked Ms. Elgnis for the job and she thought it was a *marvellous* idea" I emphasized the 'marvellous' imitating Ms. Elgnis's lofty tone. "Now, for the reason?"

She let out a sigh and returned me the badge. "The author of The Hidden Time is coming to the Glass Wing picnic as a guest. If you want to talk to him and ask him things about the book, it's the only time you'll have."

"Now that's pretty cool. Wait. You're not lying to me so that I can get motivated and read faster? Right?"

"Why would I lie to you, Cove? Investing time to make up a lie for someone is attention and interest in other forms."

Teasing someone is also a form of interest, Salem. I've just discovered her love language and can't get enough of it. The key is provocation.

"You're talking too long for someone who's

not interested."

The ceasing of movement when I said that amused me and the words that followed went straight to my heart.

"It's a risk I'm willing to take."

Salem, *you* could be my Utopia.

Chapter 13

I am wide awake, fumes coming out of my ears. I slept all day, on a Saturday. All that because of you know who. The worst in this story is the fact that there were no waffles. We waited hours; I had to listen to him blabber on and in the end, no waffles. An employee had come at the very last minute to tell us there's been a misunderstanding and the opening days had changed. These days they think if they post it on social medias everyone will know. They should have put up a flyer in front of the stand. Don't assume everyone's glued to their phone. Don't assume that everyone is welcoming the new technologies and throwing away the good old fashion things! In life, not everything has to grow and change. Some objects are perfectly fine. Fix the problems rather than creating new ones. Anyway, we weren't able to eat the waffles and truly, it was a shame. Only by looking at the pictures online, my mouth watered. I got the miniature bookshop as a consolation gift and placed it on the shelf previously occupied by Captain Bunnybeard. What to do with this bunny that smelled like the sea? He lost his home on the shelf and would need a new home. Next to the cushions on my bed is the last place I'll ever think of. Rectification: I won't even consider it. Right then, in the corner of my eye, I noticed a large surface. It wouldn't be so bad for it to be on the desk I rarely used. Placing it there would reduce the amount of times I'd need to match eyes with it. When it was on the shelf, I'd seen it when I came in the room as well as out. But truly, Captain Bunnybeard isn't an important detail to this situation. The fact is that I slept during the day. I'm fully rested, but that crazy clock on my bedside table tells me it's midnight. Being an early riser, it all made no sense. It's in my nature to sleep at a reasonable time and awake in the morning. I've missed a whole day by sitting in line and sleeping. I couldn't even go to the library. What a waste. My work week starts on Monday and ends on a Friday like many people and the weekends are for rest, which for me is going to the library as a reader. The only days I am not there are sick days. My parents were so worried they came to check on me, carrying a whole pharmacy on a tray. They didn't know what was wrong and brought everything from headache pills to cough syrup and even constipation medicine. I had to reassure them a million times, though I couldn't tell them the reason why I was tired. If my mom knew, she'd never let it go and push me to him even more. She'd hang out with Cove's mom more frequently and they'll start making wedding plans over a cup of coffee. My dad, he wouldn't say much, he'll be forced by mom to go on fishing trips with Cove's father to create a bond in advance. My mom enjoys not only to read stories of the olden ages but she likes to create her own old fashion stories. Sorry, mom, it's all make believe. Nothing will ever happen between Cove and me. It never should happen.

Seeing that I am awake at this insane time, it would do me no good to stay in bed wasting more time. I'd done that all day. Preparing for the picnic would be productive. And so I've made up my mind. Turning on the lamp on my night table, I slid down off my bed to the crimson carpet, my back to the bed. I took out from under my bed a large white box—resembling one you'd have a brand new bag in. I stole the box from my mom's closet years ago. I gathered in it all that would be useful for the picnic. Rather than having a bunch of objects with sentimental values, there were binders and notebooks. This is how I commemorated and planned. Now that the time had come to open the box and truly plan this event myself, I felt overwhelmed. My past self might have gone overboard. Papers. All I saw were papers of all sorts. There were recipes for the sweet treats we'd need to provide, a list of potential musicians to invite for the ambience, a list of the best books to put in the book lottery, a list of activities you could arrange such as a book swap and more. The urge to start anew in a fresh notebook grew as I flipped through the mountain of material. Problem is, I didn't have a new or unused notebook in my room. I could write it all on a laptop, but that just isn't my style. Pen on paper is. The smell of ink, it's faint, but it's there. The satisfaction that comes with making loops—if you write in cursive—is incomparable. At this hour, no store is open and my anger hadn't subdued yet. Cove, Cove, Cove! My sleep schedule is most probably messed up and work will be tough.

Thinking longer, I recall that there is a place where I could find an empty notebook at any hour. Though it's not the pretty kind, only a plain one with a single colour on the cover. There's a stack of them at the library for book clubs. I suppose it'll do. Midnight, being quite the odd hour to leave one's home, worried me, however, only a tad bit. My body's been idle for too long, on a camping chair or my bed. In addition to working on the picnic, I'll see Nabi. We've been apart for much too long. I've gone a full day without seeing her cute green eyes and those little paws that walked all over me. Not being able to go on any longer, I did it. I sneaked out of the house. Would you really call it sneaking out if I'm a dependable adult? I pay my part, I'm of age, and these are the only reasons I'd need to prove my point.

12:30, a time I never thought I'd be seeing on the clock of the library. Even during the day, I'd never seen it—being on my lunch break. But here I was, cheek to cheek with sweet Nabi. She was surprised to see me as well and was affectionate. Nabi pressed and rubbed her body against my legs. She followed me and never left my side. Once I sat down next to the graphic novel section with my lime green notebook, she sprung to my lap. I better come at midnight from now on to receive this kind of treatment. Now, I must focus. Nabi was a hell of a distraction, but I needed to remember that the chance of organizing a library's annual picnic is special. A deep breath followed by an exhale, and I flipped open the notebook. Skipping the first page, I went for the second. With the right supplies, I'd write up a pretty title page another day. Let's go with a brainstorming session to start. Après, we'll compile it into a brief outline. And like a cat lady, I spoke to Nabi in hopes of finding fresh ideas.

"We should have a book lottery, don't you think?"

Nabi blinked one, two, three times before ultimately closing her eyes and resting her head on my lap. I kept on talking; my voice being her lullaby. She peacefully moved her tail up and down, hitting my knee. Saying *hitting* might make it seem painful, but it was more so comforting taps.

"I wonder which book I should choose. Kids to teenagers to adults attend the event; it's hard to decide on one book that could please them all. Perhaps I should make a lottery for each age group, thus offering different books."

An idea in mind, I filled the first point on the page.

"Problem is that the range of age in the adult category is broad. Let alone the fact that everyone has different preferences. I may have to scrap the book lottery, seeing that I couldn't possibly satisfy each person."

As if she disagreed with me, Nabi readjusted herself, digging deeper into my lap.

"You're right, completely scrapping it would not be great for the event. I could let the winner choose a book from the library. That's it!"

Why didn't I think of this from the beginning? I put a line over the previous idea and wrote this one instead.

"You have something else, Nabi the muse?"

Her existence alone gave me inspiration, though it was limited.

"For the sweet treats, it was decided years ago that I'd bake my round sables with homemade strawberry jam in the middle as well as lemonade, since we have lemon trees in the library's garden."

My cookies had quite the reputation—between the library staff. I make them at least three times a year. They were officially going to make their debut this summer. And I don't doubt their municipal success. As for the lemonade, the previous director planted lemon trees since he adored lemons much as I adore strawberries. When I become director of Glass Wing, I'll plant strawberries in the garden, following in his footsteps. Still, his vision was wider than using the lemons for himself. With those lemons, we make lemonade and sell it for a small fee. And that small fee goes towards children reading programs. We even let the members of the kids' book club behind the stand for it to be a learning experience. I would have loved to be under the reign of this director. Unfortunately, he passed away before I finished my studies. He was different and much more present than our current director. He was a true librarian who didn't lose his status even after climbing to the position of director. He was a great storyteller. He was the one who introduced me to classic tales and formed my greed for reading. He's the reason I dreamed of becoming a librarian. I relate to his visions and want to keep them alive, as well as adding my own. One day, I'll become director. One day.

Just as I racked my brain for more ideas, my phone vibrated in my pocket, startling Nabi, who awoke meowing.

Unknown number:

.... . .-.. .-.. --- / .--. .-. . - - -.-- / ... .- .-.. . —

Believe it or not, I knew what it meant. This message was written in Morse code. After having seen this code in a pirate book, it became a mission of mine to get the hang of it. But I never thought it would ever be of use. I better reply to Cove's message. It is pretty obvious that it's him seeing that the message reads: Hello, pretty Salem. No one else calls me that. Moreover, I knew Cove liked pirates, but not to the extent of writing in Morse. It's the first impressive skill he showed me since coming back.

Salem:

.... --- .-- / -.. --- / -.-- --- ..- / -.- -. . --- .-- / -- --- .-. ... . / -.-. --- -.. .

(How do you know Morse code?)

Cove:

- .... . .-. . ... / .-. . .- .-.. .-.. -.-- / -. --- - .... .. -. --. /
-.-- --- ..- / -.-. .- -. - / -.. ---

(There's really nothing you can't do)

Salem:

- .... . .-. . ... / .--. .-.. . -. - -.-- / .. / -.-. .- -. - / -.. ---

(There's plenty I can't do)

Cove:

.. - / -.. --- . ... -. - / ... . . -- / .-.. .. -.- . / .. -

(It doesn't seem like it)

Salem:

.-- .... . .-. . / -.. .. -.. / -.-- --- ..- / --. . - / -- -.-- / -.
..- -- -.... . .-.

(Where did you get my number?)

Cove:

..-. .-. --- -- / .- / ..-. .- .. .-. -.-- / .. -. / - .... . / .-.. ..
-.... .-. .- .-. -.--

(From a fairy in the library)

Ms. Elgnis! It had to be her. There's
something fishy going on in the background.

He's been slowly dragging her to his side. And after all those years spent together, she leaves me for a pretty face with blond hair.

Salem:

.-- .... -.-- / -.. .. -.. / -.-- --- ..- / -- . ...- --. . / -- .
(Why did you message me?)

Cove:

-.... . -.-. .- ..- ... . / .. / -.- -. . . .-- / .-- . .-.. / -.... . / .-
.-- .- -.- . / .- - / - .... . / ... .- -- . / - .. -- .
(Because I knew we'd be awake at the same time)

Salem:

-.-- --- ..- / .-. .. .- .. -. . . -.. / -- -.-- / ... .-.. . . . .-. / ...
-.-. .... . -.. ..- .-.. . .
(You ruined my sleep schedule)

Cove:

.. ..-. / .-- . / ... - .- .-- / ..- --. / ..- -. - .. .-.. / - .- ---
-- --- .-. .-. --- .-- / -. .. --. .... -
(If we stay up until tomorrow night)
.. - .-.. .-.. / -.... . / ..-. .. -..- . -..
(It'll be fixed)

Salem:

.. / -.-. --- ..- .-.. -.. / -. . ...- . .-.

(I could never)

Cove:

-.-- --- ..- / .... .- ...- . / -- .

(You have me)

What if I really had him? What would change? Was he going to keep my eyes open all day with clothespins? Either be specific or don't say it at all. Five minutes had passed and I still left Cove hanging with that last text. It wasn't an easy one to respond to. It was no question or greeting. This message was a self-declared statement. *Self,* since he's the only one who thinks that way. I don't recall having him at all or wanting him, for that matter. But Cove wasn't the patient type; he filled the void for me.

Cove:

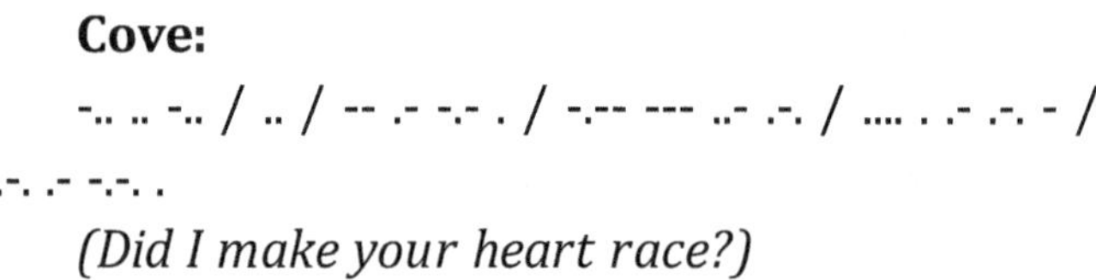

-... .. -.. / .. / -- .- -.- . / -.-- --- ..- .-. / .... . .- .-. - /
.-. .- -.-. .

(Did I make your heart race?)

Salem:

.-- .-. --- -. --. / .- -. .... -- .. .-.

(Wrong answer)

Cove:

... .. -. -.-. . / .-- .... . -. / .-- .- ... / - .... / .- / --.-
..- .. --..
(Since when was this a quiz?)
.- .-. . / -.-- --- ..- / .. -. / - .... . / .-.. .. -... .-. .- .-. -.--
(Are you in the library?)

Salem:

-. ---
(No)

I lied. I couldn't face him the way I am right now. My heart did race—a never-ending marathon.

Chapter 14

Finito, my healthy sleep schedule is over! My attempt to get a wink out of the night fell short. What did I except after having slept a full day? In the end, I read an entire book, planned the event some more, and sneaked my way back home at around five in the morning. That—productive night—won't happen again. Never. Tonight, I'll sleep at the right hour. Yes, I've decided to follow Cove's advice of staying up all day, though it'll be with my own company. There was no friendly outing planned for the day—in my knowledge. However, with Cove, you never know, and that is why I turned off my phone. Pretending to be asleep is the way to go. He wouldn't dare to come find me here. Besides, he doesn't know where I live. Or does he? Ms. Elgnis wouldn't have given him an entire file about me; that would be going too far. I am constantly in fear knowing that Cove could call anytime and I'd have no choice but to accept his outing request. What kind of agreement is this? Why aren't there any flexible terms? Twelve more outings, I think to myself... Why does the number seem so large?

Yawning and stretching my arm—pretending to have only woken up—I made my way downstairs.

"What a surprise. We even get to have breakfast with you? What's happening?" My mom said, her hands on the floral apron on her waist.

"Nothing is happening. It's a lazy Sunday for me."

A lazy Sunday for me still consisted of eating breakfast behind the library. Yet another white lie to count.

"Do you feel better?" my dad asked, his head peeking out of the newspaper he held.

"I was never sick, just tired."

My mom's right lip corner lifted and her eyes were like a hawk's when she looked at me. Shudders down my spine as I walked to the kitchen. My mom would only give me this look when she was hiding good news or when a lie of mine was crystal clear on her radar.

I rummaged through the freezer, taking out the box of frozen waffles. Putting one in the toaster, I thought of the waffles sandwiches we had failed to eat yesterday. It'll taste the same as my breakfast; I'm sure of it. And when having waffles for breakfast, I always encounter this same problem; how can I apply strawberry cream cheese on something with a honeycomb-appearance? Do you apply the spread on each little square? It's better to avoid spreads for waffles and stick to whipping cream making it the unhealthiest breakfast. I compensate by placing strawberry halves on top. Splitting the waffle, I made my very own sandwich. No need to stand in line from dawn. The finishing touch, a drizzle of honey. I heavily need all the sweetness I can intake, as this was going to be a long day. I feel those sleepless hours having a toll on me. Today, instead of the library, I'll live in a coffee shop to drink as much coffee as I can. No one drinks coffee at home, thus there's no machine. Even if there was, I wouldn't know how to use it. And I am not stepping foot in Glass Wing today. Any sighting of him will bring my life to peril.

"Sugar on top of sugar," my mom commented at the table.

She had an egg on toast while my dad had toasts with almond butter. Everyone had the task of taking care of their own breakfast. I think. I'm not here often.

"Leave her alone a bit," my dad said. "It's been a while since we ate breakfast together."

Everything's been a while for them, dinner, breakfast, what's next? Lunch, no, that was practically impossible.

"I know what you've been up to," declared my mom, making me freeze mid bite, cream oozing out both sides of the waffle.

"You do?" asked not me but my dad.

"I do."

Were they reenacting their wedding or what? Let me hear the rest! Does she really know? Is she bluffing? Is she making an assumption?

"I heard from Ms. Elgnis that you've been hanging out with Cove."

Ms. Elgnis's mouth seems to be quite loose.

"Who's Cove?" my dad chimed in, mouth full of bread and sticky almond butter.

"Isa's son."

"Who's Isa?"

"You know nothing about me." She dropped her bread back on the plate. "Isa. Isa, my best friend."

I didn't know they were *best* friends and as much as I hate when my parents fight; I hoped this one would last long enough for them to forget about the current subject, Cove and, I suppose, me. Alas, I am out of luck. My mom turned back to face me, waving the bread in her hands as she spoke.

"I even heard you were seen talking before I suggested meeting him. What's happening here?" Her cheekbones were going to hurt the next day from all the smiling she'd done.

Now, how was I going to explain this delicate situation? Two pairs of eyes were fixed on me and I sat there trying to swallow the bite that melted ever so slowly in my mouth. My white lie bank was at its limits. What do you do when reaching the limit? You take out a loan. In this situation, the loan was yet another lie, one of a bigger scale. The interest is really going to hurt.

"He loves to read and when we talk, it's about books; I'm a librarian, remember?"

I laughed internally, just thinking of the nonsense I spouted. Remembering that his mom and my mom are best friends gave me the shudders. She must know that Cove was never the bookworm type. That's why you shouldn't lie. You're so nervous that you end up saying something you didn't think twice about. A lie is found out pretty quickly when it's far from accuracy. This one is light years away from accuracy; you'd get to the moon faster.

"Isa never told me about this. She only talks of the influential school he attends."

I'm screwed. I need to inform Cove of my lie so that he can inform his mom, but she'll never believe he became a bookworm in the span of a couple days. Once again, I'm screwed.

"You see. You don't have to worry about someone else's son. He's doing fine reading books during his summer break," added my father.

"Yes, yes," my mom treated his words as flying dust and continued on, "This doesn't explain your weird schedule. You're home more often and slept during the day after coming back in the morning. Do you go clubbing?"

"I never went near a club."

"Then what is it?" she pressed. "You told us it wasn't the library."

"I-" It's ridiculous to keep lying about something so insignificant. They're friendly outings, not dates. The teasing of mom would be more painful than those outings, I fear.

New loan incoming, "I started to work out and got addicted to it. That's why I'm often too tired to go back to the library."

"Ha!" My mom let out a laugh. "I don't believe you in the least, but if I keep asking, I'll receive yet another crazy answer."

"Leave her alone. She's an adult with her own life. At least she's getting out of that stuffy library," my dad said in my defence, offending me instead.

"Don't tell me you joined a gang and go on these strange missions. It would explain your addiction to bandanas."

"They're head-scarves and do you really think I belong in a gang?"

"I'm running out of ideas," she said, bringing her plate to the kitchen.

"Your mom's quite the funny character, isn't she?" my dad said, chuckling.

"Isn't she?" I repeated, faking a smile.

I shoved the rest of my breakfast in my

mouth and joined my mom in the kitchen, waiting for my turn to use the sink.

"I hope you're not doing anything dangerous," she said, hands occupied at scrubbing her plate.

"You don't know me well enough if you think I'm putting my life in danger."

"Of course I know you. You're my daughter. What kind of mother would I be if I didn't know you?"

"Than believe in me while asking less."

I might have been a tad too harsh. My mom, though, is so strong-minded that these words wouldn't bypass the walls around her mind.

"As you like, but reconsider hanging out with Cove. Even if you say he likes to read, don't let him spend his precious summer in a library. He has no one else of his age here."

What about my precious summer? Is it only precious when it comes to Cove? I have and had no one too. I spend all my seasons with myself only.

"I'll consider it."

Perhaps I could slowly crawl out the lies with this one.

"I'm Sol, your barista for today. How may I help you?" A girl with moss-green eyes told me.

"Do you have something with plenty of caffeine to keep me awake all day but that is not too bitter and has somewhat of a strawberry flavour?"

"For this beautiful spring day; what about an iced strawberry latte? It consists of a shot or two of espresso with the milk of your choice, strawberry syrup and, of course, Ice."

"It's perfect. I'll take that with almond milk and only one espresso shot." I was overwhelmed by her enthusiasm while enjoying the sight of a passionate person. She must really like coffee.

"Does coffee go well with strawberry?" I asked to make sure.

"Personally, I only drink black coffee so I wouldn't how it tastes. But many ordered it this spring. It must be good."

I envied her for liking coffee. This fact alone made her seem more mature even though she looked close to my age. It was too bitter for me. My taste in food was of a child.

A buzz in my hand and I trembled. I'd turned my phone back on to listen to music on the way and forgot to put it on airplane mode. I was reluctant to open it. Peeking with one eye, I swiped up. Of course, it's a message from Cove. I am doomed.

Cove: We have a date tonight. Meet me in front of the library at 11 pm.

11 pm? He must be crazy to ask me out so late, I need to sleep. And the word *date* really pissed me off. If someone saw my screen, they'll misunderstand and I'll become the talk of the town. **The loner of the Glass Wing library, Salem, has a boyfriend.** He's gonna get a piece of my mind.

Salem: I work tomorrow, remember?

Cove: Let's meet at 10 then. Oh, and skip dinner tonight.

Could you kill someone through a cellphone? Somebody tell me how.

Salem: It's too much.

This text, he hasn't responded to despite having read it.

"Your strawberry latte is ready," the barista in front of me said, handing me the cold drink.

"Thank you, I'll see you again. You see, I'll need a lot of caffeine today."

"I'll be here," she said, a bright smile printed on her face.

Taking a sip of my drink, my eyes widened. The sweetness made me squeeze my shoulders up. My tongue barely noticed the espresso shot. I've never enjoyed the taste of coffee; I only ever drank it for the energy boost. It's a plus if the flavour's good. Now, I think I've found my coffee shop pick. I could see myself drinking this often.

Now out of the cherry street coffee shop, I hopped onto my bike. A bit of exercise would add to the effect of the coffee, no? It would bring me the energy I desperately needed. Then I'll drink my latte while reading a good book on a park bench. I never left the house without a book in my tote bag. Today, I'll read one of my favourite, Howl's Moving Castle.

Chapter 15

Wasn't this supposed to be a long day? How come it's already 10 pm? Time dashes at high speed. I should have been in the bathroom, getting ready for bed, but no, I am in front of a closed library. I drank four strawberry lattes to withstand the day and if our friendly outing would pass by speedily; I could fix my sleep schedule by returning to bed before the end of twilight. However, I know this outing will only dig deeper to make space for the problem. My biological clock is crying about these outings which, à propos are becoming more and more varied in time. Two of them were in the afternoon, one at dawn and this one at twilight. Can't we bring back the afternoon outings? Or better, stop them altogether.

"Pretty Salem," I hear from my left.

At this point, it's an eerie murmur coming from the ghost haunting me. If I throw salt at him, would he leave me alone?

He came running to me wearing a ridiculous grey bucket hat; It's no use when the sun had already set.

"You're always early, pretty Salem. Are you so eager to go out with me?"

He was full of himself and addicted to a nickname made by a fault of mine. I'll never forgive myself for that. He uses it as a period at the end of his sentences.

"Where are we going?"

Answering or denying his claim would only add oil to the fire and that fire is burning high enough.

"Eager. I knew it." He placed his index on his chin and his thumb under it, not bothering to hide a smile. "From my text, you probably know we're going to eat. I'm treating you tonight. I hope you didn't bring your wallet. If you did, don't you dare take it out."

This seemed more like a date, which is what scares me. I didn't want it to feel like a date. The antecedents were weird, but at least felt like friendly outings. Dinner was a classic date from the dating manuals. Or so I thought.

It's Cove we're talking about; nothing's normal about him.

The walk there wasn't long. Most things were at a walking distance in Mardi Town; the town isn't as vast as you'd think. It's full of interesting spots but it's crammed together like a large family living under a same roof. That's how I think Mardi Town is, a community living under a roof as colourful as a rainbow. Going back to the dinner, Cove certainly didn't disappoint.

"Cactus?" I told him, not believing where he'd bring me.

We were at Cactus—a Mardi Town only fast food. The last time I'd been there was for my birthday ten years ago—my parents had to beg me to come. I wanted to hide when the employees brought out their special cactus cake—a square green cake with cactus texture drawn on and around it as well and the cherry on top: googly eyes. The mascot of this restaurant—if you could call it that—is a cactus in a pot with googly eyes. He stands next to the entrance, letting the wind flap his long arms like inflatable tube dolls you'd find in front of gas stations. For me, it's more of a scarecrow than a mascot.

"What are we waiting for? Let's go in. I am so hungry I might eat that mascot," he said, rushing inside.

Please do. Please eat that mascot. I want it gone, with you included.

Well, looks like I'm overcoming a trauma today. It's not my birthday, so I won't be receiving the cactus cake nor the cactus chant. They don't sing happy birthday normally here; they sang it to me this way:

Happy birthday to you,
Happy birthday to you,
Happy birthday dear little cactus,
Happy birthday to you...

You might say that 'little cactus' goes with their concept but I think they were too lazy to remember the kid's name or learn the pronunciation of it. How embarrassing is it to be called a little cactus in a fast-food chain where people are dressed in green from top to bottom? Don't get me started on the interior... Entering Cactus at my turn, I was expecting my eyes to itch from all the lights and colours. I truly was expecting to feel my strawberry lattes to go through the tunnel in reverse mode. But the lattes hadn't switched trajectory and my eyes were intact. The place had changed since I last came. I never thought it would or could. First, the most important, the lighting was dim, and the walls were painted grey-black, making the place sombre. Next to each diner-like booth was a cactus green neon sign stuck on the wall that said 'Cactus'. This place was now more hip, which is a far cry from what I've known it to be. The audience had changed too. Normally, little kids with their parents came for a family diner here. Tonight, young people of my age were talking over hamburgers. The time—10 pm—could also be a factor to this change.

"What do you want to eat?" he asked me, already in front of the cashier.

"Did the owner of this place change?" I said, walking to the counter.

This was the only reasonable explanation; that the previous owner was an old guy who was too bright of a person, he passed away and his child who hated this place took up the challenge to transform it into a place they'd consider as a hot spot. Was this going too far? I've read so much books, it went to my head. My brain is functioning like a book. Everything has a story.

"It's been years," he answered. "Don't tell me you never came here after the renovations?" He lowered his chin until I could see it double.

My silence was his answer.

"You missed out on your youth, then. Didn't you come here with your friends after school?"

My friends were the books, and my *Cactus* was the library.

"Let's just order. Did the menu change too?"

"Kind of. I don't remember the previous menu, but fast-food is fast-food, it's the same everywhere."

"Then you choose for me. I don't mind."

Feeling a bit down, I went and picked out a booth for us. I sat on cheap green leather that felt more like a sheet of tight plastic. I sat giving my back to the door, it's awkward to match eyes with people who came in the shop. It was back then since I wore a green paper cone hat and had that hideous cake in front of me.

Cove came back with two trays, both full as can be.

"I know it says fast food, but this is too fast.

It's suspicious," I remarked.

"If you eat fast food regularly, you'll get sick. If you eat fast food merely a couple times in a year, it's not too dangerous," he said, opening the wrapper of his burger.

"You must know, after having eaten it every day with your friends."

What was this jealousy I sensed in my words? I never wanted to envy someone. Cove would be the last person I'd envy. But perhaps there was something about him that made my heart itch a little. When I think of the days I was surrounded by people of my age. When I was at the age where you had the freedom to play and laugh till you drop, I did none of those things while Cove did everything. He was loved by everyone and never spent lunch hour alone. He never had a class without a friend to talk to. While for me, it was the complete opposite. Our lives were so different, yet they've found a way to collide. It seemed so impossible, like the sun approaching the moon. With this comparison, this story feels like a fever dream. When the heat of summer passes, I'll awake from it and life will resume. The sun and the moon were not meant to be near. It would be the beginning of the end, ultimately leading to the end.

"I came, but I rarely ate their food," he said, opening the ketchup packets with his teeth.

"Your appetite was low?"

"Far from it. I was on the track team and had to be careful of what I ate. I brought homemade lunches. My friends were always laughing when I took out chicken breasts and salad."

"Were they laughing when you won medals?"

Cove removed his mouth from the burger he had yet to bite.

"No, they weren't," he chuckled lightly.

"Then you did well." I don't know why I said that...

"You wanted to comfort me. How nice of you," he said, placing a hand on my hair and ruffling it, left and right.

Despite my frown, he kept on and I thought to myself: *Why didn't I wear a headscarf today?* Yes, I let my hair out today and wore nothing on top. If I'd worn something, he'd never think to lay a hand on my head. He carefully patted down my hair that most probably turned into a mess. he'd done it with a foolish smile. The kind of smile you'd see on someone so innocent you'd think they feed on white clouds and sunshine. My heart was warmed for an odd reason. I opened the wrapper of my burger, not saying a word. I don't think I could speak now. Cove hadn't spoken either and began to eat. My heart signalled so many things at the same time that it was hard to discern any of them.

It was drunk and tried its best at organizing its thoughts. I stuffed fries in my mouth without having dipped them. My mouth being full, I couldn't possibly sputter any more nonsense that would require him to do such actions.

"Pretty Salem is even prettier when her cheeks are full," he said, having full cheeks himself.

There was no way to bypass his words or actions. He'd even say something sweet if he caught me peeing on a tree—which will never happen.

"What's wrong with you?"

Cove looked at me, his eyes dripping with honey. He placed an elbow on the table and wrapped his hand over his cheek.

"What's wrong with me?" he scoffed. "Simply say you want to hear it again. I am infatuated with you, Salem. Can't you see?"

"Infatuation isn't love, it's short-lived admiration." If I can make kids dream with stories, I can break them for adults.

"Love starts with infatuation," he said, triggering me.

"Then you won't love me as much after the infatuation stage passes."

"After infatuation comes another stage." His smile really never disappeared from his face. It only differed each time. During this conversation, it was sly. He looked like the master of a game, seeing me fall into every trap he set.

"And what is that stage?"

"Attachment. A sense of security, closeness and trust."

I fell into the carefully crafted trap. A layer covering my heart broke into pieces like glass. It was eye-opening to hear those words. I didn't know myself what came after infatuation, even after having read piles of romance novels. Fiction was fiction and in front of me was a dreamlike reality. Cove, to me, feels like that. Too good to be true, as a person and a situation. It's getting harder and harder to accept the truth. I've once had a dream where happiness was at its best and the moment I realized it was a dream, I begged myself to not open my eyes; the moment I thought it, I woke up. I couldn't fall asleep afterwards and had lost the chance of falling back into that dream. It never came back. No matter how many nights came, this same dream never returned. My memory of it faded over time till I completely forgot its content. The only memory left is the desperate moment before opening my eyes. A single second and a blue sky were also part of that memory.

"That's for people who have a future," I told him, staying loyal to my role.

Chapter 16

"You're late Salem, for the first time in your entire career as a librarian," said Ms. Elgnis.

"It will not happen again."

"Knowing the cause behind it, I wish for it to happen again. Here's your coupon for unlimited excused tardiness," she said, handing me imaginary coupons—a piece of air.

"I have some bones to pick with you, Ms. Elgnis," I said, waving my index.

She brought her head back and lifted her eyebrows. "I'm curious. You've never said something like that to me before," she said, a giddy look to her.

"I heard you were Cove's informant."

"Ah, that bone. Don't blame an old lady for wanting to see the people around her happy."

"You're not old, Ms. Elgnis,"

"I'm old enough for you to call me Ms.

Elgnis even after years of knowing each other."

I scratched the back of my neck, not being able to refute this claim. I didn't see people for their age and didn't think of Ms. Elgnis as an old lady. The way I call her is simply for manner purposes. Daily it changed. On some days, she seemed like a friend I could joke with. On others, she felt like a cool aunt I could confide in.

"You only treat yourself as old when it suits you; when it can make up for an excuse," I told her, remembering the precedents.

"What's wrong with that?" she put her tongue out, switching her age.

"Don't avoid the question. Why did you give him information about me?"

"What's so bad about him? Cove is a good boy."

"He is, but I'd rather not get attached."

"You're hiding something. I want to dig, but I'm not sure you'll allow me to."

"Nothing to dig here. I'm an open book."

Ms. Elgnis laughed so hard, she nearly tripped on her foot.

"You, an open book? I'd believe the boy who cried wolf over you. You're more closed off than you think, Salem. Every time you confide in me, I always have the feeling you leave out some words. You're a book with ripped pages that makes people go crazy."

It was rather shocking to hear this. Some parts of you are visible only to the people around and no technology out there will show you the side they see. If someone hadn't informed me about it, I would have known nothing about it. Like the dark side of the moon; nobody would have known if it weren't for scientist or astronauts. In this case, Ms. Elgnis was the scientist who revealed the secret.

Emotions and thoughts were steadily in conflict within me. It had been that way nearly all of my life.

"I make people go crazy?"

That last part sparked confusion.

"In a good way. You're not easy to read and for people who are curious souls, they'd go crazy trying to read your thoughts."

"But what if I don't want someone to read my thoughts?"

"You don't have to let everyone read your thoughts but the day will come where you will deliver them yourself—by hand—to that special someone," she gave me a wink, holding a meaning only I could decipher right before she left to the aid of a lost reader.

Will that day really come? Rather than me driving Cove crazy, it's him that's driving me crazy. Is it bad that when Ms. Elgnis mentioned a special someone, I immediately thought of Cove? I'd like to believe that it was my subconscious who acted on my behalf and it acted this way because the face it had often seen these days was Cove's. I'd like to believe there's no other reason. Lying never was my forte and to myself, it was weaker than a twig. The ripped pages of my books would be better off crumpled and thrown in the garbage. Those feelings to me are a mystery. When Cove came back after three years, the feelings hadn't returned with him. I didn't think of him that way anymore. My crush for him in high school was more so admiration rather than love. An innocent crush it was. Now, as an adult, I am developing something stronger and it's terrifying. What if one day I think I can't help myself anymore and let my last bit of morale go? What if I ran to him? Cove implanted a new fear in me. I hate him for that. We're not meant to be together and I'm not talking of destiny, I'm talking of distance and people. We're both different and have different entourages. He'll be surrounded by college students all day and I'll be in this library. He'll have the opportunity to meet all kinds of people and when we are faced with new things, changes are inevitable. I'm scared of changes. That's probably why I spend my days the way I do. Though this summer, my routine drastically changed. At first, it was hell on earth, however with time, it had its charms. Last night at that fast-food chain, I felt comfortable yet tickled. Throughout all the outings, comfort and stability were both there. I don't have to keep an eye out when I'm with him. My heart craved that peace of mind. Soon I'd need to find an alternative. As I was falling into a rabbit hole of possible alternatives, the answer came to my feet. Nabi pressed her paws on my shoes, making me melt to the floor. On other thoughts, I shouldn't think of her as an alternative. She came before Cove and has a place of her own in my heart, though she always forgets to pay the rent and the utility fees. Just like there is no alternative to Nabi, there seems to not be any alternative to Cove. In my lifetime, there can only be one man who waltzes in the library and suddenly confesses his love to me. That one opportunity itself was a miracle. Things don't just happen. To find someone, I'd need to make an effort. My luck ran out. Was it luck if it walked away? Cove reminds me of a Glass Wing. He's like a rare butterfly that shows off the beauty of its wings and flies away with them, leaving the memory of it engraved in your brain. The previous director liked it so much he named the library after it. He must have been reminded of that butterfly every day. When he saw the sign or when he went to their meeting place. I enjoy the fact that I resemble the previous director, but the situation is odd. Because of him, I'll see the Glass Wing as Cove and remember him for as long as I work here —which means, till death. Before I knew it, a tear escaped my eye, going directly for the burgundy carpet where a spot darkened. Then came another from the other eye. Our carpet wasn't safe anymore. Nabi nudged my legs, shifting from one to the other. I patted her back a few times before running to the bathroom. It wasn't a scene to flaunt. Even to myself, in front of the mirror, it looked pathetic.

***

"I finished the book!" Cove said, running to me.

My heart broke at the sight, though I didn't show it.

"Which book?"

"The hidden Time," he said, settling by my side.

"Didn't you only start it on the weekend?"

"Sunday night, right after our date at Cactus."

I didn't correct him this time, not that I'd lost my motive, but I lacked the energy to do so.

"That book ate you alive."

I knew that he'd have a breakthrough with this reading list. There's always this one book that you get so invested, it changes your perspective on reading and turns you into a bookworm. For Cove, it might have been this one. He'll surprise everyone by devouring novel after novel. This was my aim from the start. Once he starts reading regularly, he'll be stuck in his own world and forget about mine. He won't have the time to remember our deal concerning the friendly outings.

"I couldn't put it down. I read page after page and to know that I'll be able to meet the author. Wow! I have so much to ask him. When's the picnic?"

I don't know if I was imagining from the tone of his voice but all I saw was a puppy jumping and barking around. His mouth kept going off while his blond hair bounced.

"I didn't know we could learn these kinds of lessons in a fiction novel?" he asked.

"What lesson did you learn from this novel?"

"While there are some things that should not be lost in time, some other things are better left in the past. It's not necessarily the way up to the future, but the way home and the way out."

The way home and the way out. It's a line from the book. Just as you begin your day at home—your shelter—you go out into the day —into the future. At the end of your day you come back home, which was your beginning and perhaps you reflect on the day that has become your past. And every single moment has been your present.

"It made me want to do a time capsule just like in the book," he said, eyes flickering with sparks of light.

In the novel, a band of pirates go on adventures to leave behind a treasure for newer generations of pirates—It's basically a time capsule. The purpose of it was to maintain some pirate traditions, for them not to get lost in time. During their journey at sea, they dive deeper on their traditions and realize that some were not to be kept as they'd lost meaning in the new age and some, were perfectly fine and had no reason to disappear —it would be a significant loss. This novel has lessons everyone should learn from.

"What would you put in your time capsule?" I asked him.

"I have no clue. Contrary to those pirates, I'm not passionate enough about something to include it in my time capsule."

"Then why would you say that you want to make a time capsule?"

"The idea of it tickled my brain. What would you put in yours? Give me an example."

"I'd put in books," I said, without a hint of hesitation. "Thought I'd have a hard time deciding which book I'd leave."

"Who would you leave them for?"

"For my future self, who else? It'll be a gift

to myself. I'll reminiscence on the reading taste of younger me and have a cozy time in front of a fire in the living room."

"Wouldn't you leave them for your grandchildren?"

"I'll have no grandchildren since I'll never get married."

Marriage was never in my mind whether I'd found true love or not. I plan to spend my days in the library and my 'true' love will not walk in here. I'll keep experiencing love with romance novels. That's more like it. Isn't it?

"Don't say things like that. Emmie and Lin will get upset."

"Who's Emmie and Lin?"

"Now they're even more upset. They're our future grandchildren, the ones who'll open our time capsules."

Picking up a large book from a near shelf, I swung it at him, right at his back. He ran away, and I followed, still aiming his back. What nonsense is this? Who is he to decide on the names of our grandchildren and who is he to decide we'll have grandchildren together? I didn't feel bad while hitting him and I didn't do it lightly. I wasn't here to play anymore. We ran round the shelves until we've reached the end of the library. It annoyed me even more that he'd maintained a smile throughout the ride. He even laughed, letting a sound coming directly from his chest. A series of giggles stolen from a rainbow. That's why rainbows don't laugh, it's because Cove stole their voice. I felt myself falling into that laughter, so much that I dropped the book.

"I'm sorry, don't hit me anymore," he said, catching his breath.

Even then, his smile was painfully bright. Triangles formed on top of his cheekbones, under his eyes, while his full set of teeth was right there for me to see. I liked how sharp and triangular his teeth were; it was charming. What happened to me? Now I'm even attracted by his teeth. I picked up the book from the floor and used the need to bring it back as an excuse to...Run away from him. It's all I've been doing since the first time he set foot in the library. Who knew I'd still be at it weeks after? Honestly, who knew we'd be in contact? It was supposed to be a onetime-only awkward meeting with someone from the past. He wasn't supposed to come back every day, and I wasn't supposed to offer him a deal that made us spend time together. None of this should have happened. If I could, I'd go back in time and avoid him till death. I'd make sure we'd have no chance to even cross eye for a milli second.

"Don't run from me," he said, startling me from behind.

I didn't even hear him coming and wondered if he'd read my mind. I walked away, but he saw it as running away. The only thing on my mind now is to turn around and throw my arms around him. Would he read that too? For once, I'd forbidden my mind to control my body. Let's not make it worse than it already is. I admit it, I'm falling for Cove and hiding that would be a real task. I just need to hold out till the end of the summer, that's it.

Chapter 17

"Today, I'm letting you choose the outing. Do choose something that has to do with reading. I am enjoying it these days," Cove said, holding his hands behind his back.

We're making progress in operation *'get Cove to fall in love with reading so that he falls out of love with me'* is going along like wildfire. From another perspective, it's bittersweet.

"So?" he said, sticking his face in front of mine.

"W-we c-could read somewhere."

Someone help me; why did I stutter?

"Right, but where? I told you to choose today."

"If I choose, does this outing count towards our deal?"

He grinned, "of course, I'm not a scammer."

He talks like this is a business deal and our

time is money, whereas I don't really know what kind of deal we have. I wouldn't say we're friends or anything else. This deal is only the solution to shake him off my tail. What would it be for him? A simple challenge to his pride? I'd provoked it—his pride. Men sometimes are as simple as that. Not all, but a majority. What would I know about men? Before Cove, I only met them through fiction books. Maybe I'm not fit to talk about them. The saying that men are as simple as that was in fact told to me by Ms. Elgnis, she has much more experience than me. Anybody would have. The elementary kids of today have gone through relationships and breakups while I have yet to go on an official date—the friendly outings don't count.

"Earth to Salem. Where are we going? A chance like this doesn't come often. If you don't want it, I get it."

"No, no, I want that chance."

Here I was getting lost in an internal monologue, as always. Habits die hard. And I had an idea of where we could go read. Ever since I've seen a picture of it, it became a fantasy of mine. While surfing the net for aesthetic pictures to print out—book-related for decorating the library—I stumbled upon one of a couple laying on the grass both holding a book in their hands while in front of them was a view to die for; it was a lake whose water sparkled, reflecting rays of sunshine. From afar, you could even see a small boat passing by the calm waters. The picture itself looked so peaceful and romantic. When you use the word romantic, it doesn't necessarily mean love. You can romanticize an environment and or a situation. Our outing wouldn't be the *romantic* you'd think of. It would be something else. I don't know how to explain it, but it's different. Vastly.

"We can go read by Lupin lake, it's pretty out today."

"Sure, I need to find a book to bring first."

"What about the list?"

He smiled a cheeky smile, bringing his lower lip up high. "I finished everything on the list. I think I'm having a reading fever."

Progress, progress, progress! I can't believe it's actually working.

"Do you need help with choosing your book?"

Librarian mode on!

"For the fun of it, I'll go roam the shelves

alone," he said, bouncing away to the shelves.

It's working, he's going off alone. He's leaving me out. Books are making their place in his heart. Soon enough, they'll take my place, kicking me out. That's great! I should go look for my book as well. The rising excitement made me want to start a new book to keep that excitement going. This time, I'm going to read a book I haven't heard of; one I haven't even flipped through once. I wonder if there is still such a book in this library? I walked without a destination in my mind and left it up to fate to find me a book. The shelf I ended up walking into was the holiday romance one—yes, we have a shelf for holiday romance books. I was against it, but it's the current director's preference. Why couldn't she have made a whole Danielle steels shelf ? That would have been much better. When I'm director—that day will come, I believe it as much as I believe the sun will rise again tomorrow—I won't make shelves according to my preferences. I will keep it neutral and diverse with no bias. That's what a library is for. It's a place for everyone and shouldn't be personalized to fit a single person or a group of people. I'll take care of that shelf later and I can't believe fate has such a taste. I'll give it a second chance. Closing my eyes, I blindly went to another shelf, but I bumped into something. It wasn't hard, and it didn't hurt, thus it couldn't have been a shelf. It was soft and smelled like baby powder. Opening my eyes, I am faced with a grinning Cove.

"I left you alone for a minute and you're already looking for me. You miss your home that much?"

"Home?"

It's true that he felt warm as a home and I didn't want to take a step back, but I had to. I had to, but he didn't let me. The minute I attempted to step back, he put a hand around my waist, trapping me. Soon after, he put the other, intertwining his hands behind my back. I was so close that I heard his irregular heartbeat. Mine had either stopped or pounded like an angry neighbour with a noise complaint.

"Yes, home," he said, his voice somehow relaxed and an octave lower. "I want to become somewhat of a shelter to you, Salem. Coincidentally, my name means shelter."

Oh, how I wanted to believe these words. I did for a split second. The warmth being given to me went up to my head. I wanted to rest my head on his chest and wrap my arms around him as well. There was nothing else I wanted at that instant. Though I knew it would be a great mistake. And I don't make mistakes, well I try not to as a human being. Those words he said, I never knew how much I wanted to hear them. It was a first for me to receive words as sweet. In his arms, I feel like there's nothing to be afraid of. Nothing can happen in a butterfly's cocoon. With my hands, I tried to free myself from the cocoon. Alas, he gripped on tighter each time. This time it was like a snake tightening the grip on his prey.

"If someone sees us, they'll misunderstand!"

"There is no misunderstanding here. Soon, this will become a daily occurrence. You don't know how long I waited to hold you in my arms."

"And I don't remember telling you that you could."

I continued to struggle while he remained unfazed, not showing a sign of struggle. In reality, I fought with myself. With the urge to embrace him and the rationality to break free.

***

Cove had let go first—I saw it as a premonition—and we'd rid our bikes of their chains in front of the library, making our way to the lake.

"How refreshing," Cove said, feeling the wind bringing his blond head of hair back.

Yes, how refreshing for my heart to break for the first time. There is a first for everything, love and heartbreak. Seeing Cove, I wanted to enjoy the summer we have, knowing it'll be our last and honestly first. I've never *stumbled* upon him at the supermarket on summer break—he's the type to hang out at the skate park with his friends while I never stepped foot near it. Maybe accepting this developing love to then face the consequences at the end would be an option. I could end up regretting not taking a hold of this opportunity. Let's observe this Glass Wing butterfly a while more before it takes its flight.

"Isn't it?" I respond, accepting the wind that relentlessly hit.

"Oi, don't close your eyes. Look at the road," Cove said, leaning his arm out to tap my shoulders.

Letting go of all my worries, I felt lighter than a feather; the wind added to it and made me lose my mind—in a good way, so much that I let go of things I probably shouldn't have let go of.

"Oi? Since when do you use Oi?" I said, regaining control of the road.

"I picked it up from a book."

"Did I already turn you into a bookworm? I was suspicious when you asked me to choose a book-related outing."

"They say you pick up habits from the one you like."

I accepted his comment and allowed my lips to curve. My worries flew away—remember? Still, habits die hard and I hid my face. The wind helped me by blowing my hair to the front. Why did his hair go back while mine went forth? It went in my eyes, my mouth, ears and simply everywhere. It didn't caress my face; it battled with it like two cats would, endlessly flapping their paws.

"You okay over there?" Cove asked, noticing my battle.

"This is why I tie my hair when riding a bike."

"Let's stop then for you to attach your hair.

It can be dangerous if you can't see ahead."

Thus, we pressed on the brakes and stopped at a little bus stop with glass walls and a two-seat bench. I rummaged through my tote bag for a hair band and strangely enough, there weren't any. The only thing close to it was a foliage patterned fabric headscarf. I could use it as a hair tie, though it'd be hard to attach it by myself. Putting my hair up would be as bad as leaving it out, since the wind will bring that ponytail to my eyes with ease. I'd need to tie it down for it to stay put. I held the scarf beneath my hair; when I tried to make a knot, it fell apart with strands going outside the fabric.

"You need help, don't you?" Cove said.

He saw it all happen from the side, standing with his arms crossed.

"You know how to tie hair? And with a headscarf?"

"I have a sister, I've done it all, tying hair is nothing." He uncrossed his arms and entered through the glass door, taking a seat next to me.

My heart had already started the tambourine.

"Turn around," he said, taking hold of my

hair ever so gently. He gathered every strand of hair, brushing the skin near my face. I'm sure he did it on purpose, and I don't need to turn around to see that grin.

"I love your olive green hair."

"It's fading," I replied, in a voice quieter than usual.

I was nervous from my head to my toes. When someone touches your hair, it already feels good, but imagine how it feels when it's the person you like.

I hope the goosebumps I have don't rise to the back of my neck, or else I'll be caught.

"There's still some green to it," he added. "This colour. It fits you."

Thank you for ruining my favourite colour, Cove. When he's gone, I'll be reminded of this line every time I see something olive green and I won't dye my hair again; I'll let the colour fade completely.

"Could you pass me the scarf?"

It was a shame for it to almost be over. I liked the ticklish feeling; I felt like his fingers were little butterflies playing in my hair. I sure love butterflies for me to mention them whenever I can.

"And it's done," he said, giving the finishing

blow; he patted down my hair from the top of my head to the end of it.

I wanted to kill him while at the same time ask him to tie make this a daily occurrence.

"Thank you. Now let's go."

I couldn't turn my head and give him the satisfaction of seeing me blushing. Never. I'll enjoy the rest of the summer, but I won't let him do the same.

Chapter 18

I never thought I'd get a taste of peace in Cove's company. The world proved me wrong and now I'd believe it if you said pigs could fly. We sat on the bare grass—pants can always be washed—with books in our hands. We were right on the edge of the lake. If I were to roll on the grass, I'd roll right into the lake. That's to say, the distance between us and the lake is dangerously close. I wouldn't roll on the grass; I never did. I spent my childhood in a library while others I guess rolled in fields.

The flow of the water was our music without the lyrics. Water was an instrument needing no one to play it. Its natural sound blessed the ears of whoever lent their ears to it. To water, I gave my ears, to the pages filled with ink, my eyes, to the wind, my skin and to Cove, my attention. My eyes weren't on him, but my mind was overly conscious of his presence. Yet again, he distracted me from my favourite activity. I had a book in front of me, yet I hadn't flipped a page for a full five minutes. Cove must think I am crazy slow at reading. Was the student overpowering the master now? Was I going into a reading slump while he was entering a reading fever? No. It was all temporary. A fever doesn't last. He'll go back to his world and I'll go back to mine when this summer ends. It will all cool down.

"Why is it called the Lupin lake?" Cove said, not blinking an eye or flipping a page.

I have to admit; I jumped and closed my book in the midst.

"Is it the lake of thieves? Was it stolen?" he continued on with his silliness.

"How can you steal a lake? Do I need to teach you everything about Mardi Town? Didn't you grow up here? You've only been away for three years; the rest of your life, you spent it here."

"I wasn't interested back then. Nowadays, I find myself enjoying the little things in life. Don't know why though," he said, closing his book as well.

"Maybe you feel refreshed after having

lead a busy life elsewhere. It's not you who's noticing the little things, it's them. They're embracing you."

He smiled at the lake, who for him seemed to shine a tad brighter.

"Aren't you going to answer my question about the Lupin lake?"

I sighed, "Alright then, you should know by now that the people of Mardi Town enjoy simplicity."

"Is it something like the Glass Wing?"

"Similar. There's this flower called Lupin, and it grows on the other side of the lake. The wind takes its petals to the water and they end up floating all around."

"Really? So if I go look in the lake, I can see flower petals?"

"Surely you could. It's the season of flowers."

Cove jumped on his feet. I've never seen a man so excited to see flowers. Right then, he took my wrist and brought me nearer to the lake.

"What do you think you're doing?" I told him.

That didn't stop him as he took me farther. By farther I mean into the lake. The water wasn't shallow, thus we could walk. That cold feeling on my skin left me quiet. I should have screamed, but the shock was too grand.

"Woo!" Cove let out, splashing water with every step.

He still held on tight to my wrist and brought me on his little adventure. His spontaneous choice made me realize once again how weird of a person he is. Who in their right mind would jump into a lake with their clothes on?

"Let's look for the petals."

"We could've used our eyes for that. There was no need to enter the water. It's freezing!" Lake water was never hot.

"I'm enjoying the little things in life. It would be a waste to use my eyes only."

"Why drag me then? I've enjoyed enough little things."

"That's what you think. You've seen nothing, pretty Salem."

Here it came again, the words I despised so much. But there's been a change of 180 degrees. Hatred turned into flutter. The nickname I wanted to rip out of his mouth turned around in my head. My heart now skipped a beat every time he'd mention it. It hurts my pride to find myself enjoying a nickname that took less than five seconds to think of.

"So, what do you say we look for these petals?"

Why does it seem like I can't refuse him anything? Starting from our deal, sometimes his outing requests were a bit crazy and since we weren't bound by a contract, I could have refused. Not once did I refuse. There's something wrong with me. I can't pinpoint it.

"You're lucky to be wearing short," I said.

"Lucky? Huh, I'm even colder."

"Think in the long term. When we get out of the water, my pants will stick to my skin and I'll have it worst."

If his head is in the present, mine's in the future.

"Haven't thought about that. Sorry."

He was quick to apologize, making him lose sincerity.

"We're already in the water. It's worth a try, no? I'd be a waste to leave."

I shook his hand off my wrist and walked, keeping my eyes on the water for some petals. I'd hate to directly admit he was right. I'd also hate to see a smirk on his face. Every step was heavy, and I gave up on trying to hold up my pants. They already stuck to the skin. He could have warned me and I would have rolled them up to my knees. Mr. I live in the moment doesn't think ahead.

"You know, we could have easily seen and even scooped some petals from the grass. The wind takes them to us, not the opposite."

"When you said that the little things were noticing me, I wanted to return the favour and embrace them as well."

Since when was he such a sentimental person? My words were but mere words far from reality. I scoffed at his remark but followed through with his intention of returning that favour. Doesn't it seem like the roles changed? Normally, I'd be all about nature and he'd be all about...Me. Now I'm getting cocky. But that's really all he talked about—his interest for me. Now that I notice, Cove hasn't been talking as much about himself or his days out of Mardi Town. Heck, I don't even know what kind of studies he'd done the past three years. It was unfair for him to know quite a few pages of my book while his was out of reach.

"Hey, where's your head at?" he said,

rushing to my side. "The petals almost passed by you."

He bent down to scoop the small purple petals, water seeping through the cracks between his fingers.

"See, we found the pretty petals." He brought his hand near my face, giving me a closer look.

At that moment, I couldn't care less. My mind was preoccupied with everything about Cove. We'd gotten closer, we talked casually; we bickered, and it was fun but now it felt like I gave him my name while he kept his a secret.

"Pretty," I said, reaching into a deep place in my soul for a piece of enthusiasm to show.

It seems I'd convinced him, seeing that his expression remained the same—the joker. I refuse to believe that smile of his isn't carved on his face.

"Let's go back now; it is cold," he said, taking my wrist, again, without warning.

I let myself get dragged and didn't mind that his touch was cold and wet from all the waving he did underwater. And of course, it only got worse out of the water. It felt like I peed myself. My pants were glued to my legs, leaving a sticky and sharp feeling on my thighs.

Now, I really wanted to scream. I bit my lips to not scream. Cove's shorts were cotton and didn't stick as much as mine. I looked at him, burning with anger and, at the same time, envy. All I wanted to do was to take off my pants. That sticky feeling drove me mad.

"Cove." The only thing I could mutter was his name and I presume my face spoke other words on my behalf.

He sympathetically looked at me, taking a hold of both of my hands.

"I'm really sorry. I'll think ahead next time."

That is, if there is a next time.

"The only solution I have now is to lay on the grass and let the sun dry us."

"Yes, and let the grass dye my pants green," I hadn't screamed those words. For a strange reason, his hold on my hands calmed me down and I waved a white flag.

As he said, we laid on the grass and I envisioned myself hand washing that pair of pants with all sorts of products. I heard a mixture of hydrogen peroxide and dish soap makes wonders for grass stains.

"Close your eyes, feel the sun and let your mind drift away," he said, a voice inching towards a whisper.

"Don't let your mind wander too far. In other words, don't fall asleep. I don't want to hear any snoring," I warned him.

"Say that to yourself, pretty Salem. I can't sleep without Strawbunny in my arms. What's new with Captain Bunnybeard? He's still on the shelf."

"Nope, I moved him to put the miniature bookshop."

"So you finally caved in and brought Captain Bunnybeard to your bed?"

"Not even in your wildest dreams. He's on my desk, one brisk movement from my part and he falls into the garbage bin next to it."

"You're taking a hostage now? You never fail to disappoint me."

"You better behave if you want to see your Captain Bunnybeard again. And I really need to ask, why the scent of the sea? Because of you, my room smells like sea salt."

"Now I am curious about how your room smells like."

"I just told you how it smelled like. Salt! When I wake up, I sometimes think that a fish market was installed near our house and I'd forgotten to close the window the night before."

"Now you're exaggerating. The only way I could verify your claim is by visiting you."

We both laid with eyes closed, but the sugary tone of his voice says it all.

"Never."

"You can come to my house anytime," he said.

"Never," I repeated.

I had my reasons to be so adamant.

"Here you go, making walls around yourself again."

"Here you go, uselessly knocking on them. Your knuckles are too weak for my walls."

"I don't think so. The structure is becoming unstable and soon, cracks will form and I can use them to make an entrance."

"Who says the structure is unstable?"

"Your actions."

Though I didn't exactly recall moments where my actions spoke on my behalf, I'd have to admit the structure indeed turned weak. Cove's knuckles are definitely not weak. They've been pounding at my walls since day one. One by one, they fell like dominoes. No one could have predicted that Salem, the girl stuck in a world of her creation, would be brought out to the real world in such a short period of time. It won't be for long, though. I have a foot in each world and at the end of the summer, I'll take back that foot stolen by Cove.

"There's something I need to tell you, Salem."

He didn't use my nickname, meaning it must be something a little more serious. He's already confessed ages ago. What's left? A marriage proposal? I'd kill him before he'd finish proposing.

"Tomorrow, I'm going away."

My heart sank.

"I'm going on a father-son fishing trip for three days."

My heart floated.

"Good riddance," I told him, feeling somehow relieved.

"You won't say that when facing the world by yourself for three days. I'm sure you'll feel the most empty you've ever felt in your whole life. I will haunt your mind even from far away."

"Stop with the scary stories. I'll spend three happy days."

"We'll see," he said.

Chapter 19

I hate how right he was. A day in already and the world feels void. Like every morning, I hopped on my bike and went to the library. Nabi greeted me at the door and everything had felt normal until I sat at my station. My eyes went to the glass doors, waiting for them to be opened by Cove like he always did. I knew he wouldn't come today, tomorrow and the day after, yet I looked. And I couldn't hide the disappointment when someone else opened those doors. He messed up my mind. How could I be this way?

"Where's Cove, today?" Ms. Elgnis asked, dropping a pile of books on my desk. "Did you two stay up late again? You have to wake up early for your job but him, I suppose he's free to sleep in."

"He's on a fishing trip with his dad." I said,

taking care of the books. Then it hit me.

"Wait. How do you know we stayed up late the other night?"

"It was just a guess; turns out I was right. You were with Cove that night."

I keep on digging my grave. Hasn't it reached the bottom yet?

"How did you know?" I could learn a thing or two from Ms. Elgnis' way.

"That day you clocked in at a later time; it isn't like you. On stormy days, you took precautions to arrive at least an hour earlier. In this case, your storm must have made it impossible for you to take precautions." She kept winking as if something was stuck in her eye.

Her justification wasn't wrong, though. Cove is a storm. And like all storms, he'll pass. He'll move to another region and swipe someone else off their feet, leaving mine to be back on the floor.

"I hope you're not misunderstanding anything. There is nothing going on with Cove and I."

"You think you can fool me?"

"I am not trying to."

Her eyes drooped and lost their

playfulness. The grimace on her face took a turn.

"Don't look at me like that," I told her.

"Salem, a book isn't written to remain close."

"I'm still young and Cove isn't the only love interest I'll have in my life."

"Think like that and you'll end up like me. 69 and still single."

"You haven't been that way all your life."

"You're right. I had my fair share of love, though most of my experiences were mediocre for the exception of one which I was foolish enough to let go of. To this day, regret floods my mind. If I could, I'd go back in time and hold that hand he reached out to me. A guy like him only came once to me."

I understood her words loud and clear, but I believed everyone lived differently. Everyone had their share of adventures and happenings. Some may marry a couple of times in their lifetime and may have felt true love in each of their marriages, while some may feel none in countless relationships. What happened to Ms. Elgnis may not necessarily happen to me. That was my brain speaking, not my heart.

The day worsen with the passing time and

the real void appeared in his stead. The library grew quiet as it was before. The only actual noise came from the children, but they didn't come in till the afternoon. I picked up a book and found myself picturing Cove as the main character of it. Any book I chose, he was the protagonist. The author had specified that this person had a long black hair with no visible curls while I saw Cove's blond and curly hair. They wrote that he has a prominent jawline while I saw the fuller face of Cove. They mentioned he had dark brown eyes while I imagined azure blue eyes, just like Cove's. If I continued to read, I'll even see the female character with Cove's characteristics. And so, I dropped the book and worked extra hard to fulfil my duties as a librarian. I performed an impromptu inventory of the books, well, part of it; counting them all would take days. I took care of the graphic novels section and the children's books. Then there was the list of books whose due date had passed but were yet to be returned. I'd need to send mail notices. We like to do it the old fashion way here. Instead of being notified by email or text, we send them directly a letter written on a typewriter. Mardi Town is the kind of town that likes to be stuck in the past. What I've mentioned might be taken negatively, as it could be seen positively. See as you please since both ways are true. Other duties I have would be managing the budget and making right use of it. I've been a librarian for merely three years, but I already have my hand on the budget. I gained the trust to do so quite early on. They had no reason to doubt me and never did. As of the moment, there wasn't any budget planning to do since it was done at each quarter. I couldn't do it at the impromptu like a book inventory. Aside from all these duties, the only one I could do was the reading list making one. That's right, I often make seasonal or other themed lists to aid people into finding interesting books—ones that fit their interests. I usually post them on our blog and on the bulletin board at the entrance. I had to occupy myself with whatever I found. Those lists weren't urgent since the board was already full. I'd have to replace existent ones, which were pretty recent themselves. It was hard for a librarian to get...Busy. No wonder my parents worry. It's true the work is minimal and the future of books and libraries is uncertain, even in this old fashion town. The funds given to us by the town are getting smaller every year. The public sector itself is being minimized while the private sector is growing. One day, perhaps for the survival of Glass Wing, we might have to go private. How would that even work? A public library turned private. Would we sell the books or offer a monthly membership? That goes against our wishes to make reading accessible for everyone. Enough of this tangent that is years early. The only way for me to enter a bubble free from complicated thoughts was reading, but somehow, Cove managed to pop it. All I wanted was to get so busy that my mind won't have the time to drift. Then came to mind the picnic. The preparations were going well. I'd convinced the author of 'The Hidden Times' to come. I'd arranged for a band to come and I'd organized the book raffle. I plan to bake the cookies the night before for freshness purposes and make the lemonade the day of, in the morning. All that was left was a trip to the market for ingredients, decorations and, I suppose, utensils and glass bottles. This task was to be done when the picnic neared; around a week earlier. Sadly, the time period between today and the picnic was larger than a week. Either way, I was still hours away from clocking out and needed to stay in the library. I never minded the long hours because I spent them in a library. Being surrounded by books made me happy and complete. At least I thought so. A taste of what we call a social life and I started to crave it. I'm like a baby vampire who tasted blood for the first time. Though I'm different from vampires; I have the chance to retreat before it's too late; before the cravings consume me whole. Eating out with someone, spending hours outside, doing activities I would have never done by myself brought the speck of a light to my heart. If I can persuade my heart to turn off this light, then everything will be back to normal. I'd prefer to keep walking alone on a road where the world is behind me. You'd have to be crazy to refuse the light. But I'll go crazier after the light leaves. If this goes on and I keep opening up to him, I'm afraid I'll be scarred for life at the end of this summer. I'll never let someone in again, by fear they'd leave me. Forcing myself to spend these three days normally is the way to go. When Cove comes back, things will have to change.

"It's just me and you, Nabi," I said to Nabi,

who leaped to my desk. "No one else."

I held her in a tight embrace while she remained still, as if she understood what I was going through. She hadn't thrown her paws at me or flung her tail on my face. Nabi stood by me.

***

Restart. That's what I did for the remaining days without Cove. I've paid attention to the little things and fell in love with romanticizing my lonesome life. I bought new pens and started to colour code my notes I now carefully jot down on my reading notebook. That brought back a certain joy in reading. I bought flowers at the morning market. I found the most delightful Irises. These purple flowers were the perfect addition to my desk, which, to be honest, was plain boring. There was no romance in my life. Now's the time to bring this kind of romance. I took the initiative to go on walks during my breaks rather than staying in the library. I used my bike for purposes other than to commute. I smiled at strangers and said "hello", "Good day" to a few. It doesn't seem like much, but the change was refreshing. It gave me hope. If I keep my distance and continue this way, I might be able to forget Cove. He's a butterfly anyway.

Chapter 20

Cove's point of view

I love my dad, but the past three days have been the worst—for different reasons. Salem was one, alongside an uncertain future. Fishing is patience and long conversations with the person next to you. Instead of catching fishes, my father caught me with his never-ending questions and speeches concerning the future of society and how my major in economy will be extremely beneficial for me in the coming years. He talked about his college days and repeatedly mentioned how much he envied me. There was nothing to envy. Not a gram of me was rejoicing over there. Coming back to Mardi Town, the sun in me came back. The moon made it so. Astronomically, it doesn't make sense; were details ever important? The sun and moon will soon be reunited after three long days, which felt like months. In space, that time would have been different. Either shorter or longer.

When my dad parked the car, I leapt out and when straight to the library. From a distance I could hear my dad yell:

"Aren't you going to help me with the fishing gear and the bags? Aren't you going to greet your mom?"

The guilt I had for ignoring his words didn't compare to my yearning to see Salem. With a priority on my mind, I ran. I hadn't run in a while for the simple reason that it made me sad. It brought back memories I could never go back to. Today, I'd forgotten all about why I didn't run anymore and thought of only one—pretty Salem. At eleven in the morning, she'd probably be sitting at her station, a book in her hands waiting for lunch break. I sprinted, my smile slowly coming back. On that fishing trip, there wasn't much to smile about. Here, with the thought of her, all I can do is smile. That's all I'm planning to do. I flung the door open, scaring a little kid in the process. He was standing next to the door and was on the verge of tears. Bending down, I patted his red cap.

"I'm sorry, little kid, I was too excited to come in here. I'm not a weird person."

He wasn't on the verge of tears anymore but looking at me; he grimaced. I guess saying I'm not a weird person makes me a weird person. I left him alone, in fear he'd go find his mom and she'd call the police on me. All I did was open the door, using a lot more force than intended. On second thought, I'd be frightened as well. With the same excitement that made me open the door, I ran to Salem's station.

"Pretty Salem!" I shouted. "I missed you. Did you?"

She was having a reading session, a scarf with strawberries on that covered part of her head. When she'll lift her head, I'll officially feel like I'm back.

She brought her nose out of the book and looked at me with eyes missing their gleam. They were as empty as they were the day I came back from college.

"You're back," she told me, her tone stale.

Did I miss something? Did a feeling-catching tornado pass by while I was gone? Had the town turned dystopian? Did the government start spouting nonsense such as 'emotions are the disease'? I am definitely not over reacting. Salem's face had undergone a sort of change. By her eyes, I could tell. I've stared at them long enough before to know how they work.

"So, did you miss me?" I tried again.

"I'm busy," she replied, avoiding the question.

The Salem I knew would have responded either with sarcasm or complete rejection. Seeing her answer was nowhere near worried me to death.

Another conspiracy theory came to mind; this was a clone. They replaced citizens with clones, and I barely escaped the process by being away.

"What are you busy with? Reading a book? That's not part of your work."

"If you think so," she said, putting back her nose into the book, ignoring me, with no visible remorse.

Again, this was odd. Salem should have been offended by my claim. She should have stood from her chair, furrowed her brows, and refrained herself from shouting in the library to say that reading is very important for a librarian. This was different. Even more than the first day. I became dust in front of her.

"Earth to Salem. Are you okay?"

"I don't know what you're talking about," she said, not lifting her head.

These are the words of an AI. Either she read some dystopian books lately and was deeply immersed or one of my conspiracy theories was right.

The last test:

"You're up for a date tonight?"

I surveyed her as she paused the hand about to turn a page, but it was only for a split second.

"Sure."

That's it. She didn't complain or correct the term.

In the air flew stuffy particles. The environment of Glass Wing changed as soon as its moon shifted. The orbiting moon seemed to have darkened, and only the sun could help it by sending more light. As much as I want to keep seeing her, even with that emotionless expression, I'm afraid I have to retreat and form a plan.

"I'll text you the details," I told her and received only a nod from her part.

I couldn't hide the disappointment and

didn't need to since her eyes had only been on mine for a quick second earlier. My shoulders moping the floor, I walked away. I turned in hopes I'd caught her breaking character. Sadly, this was no acting; it was real. Was anyone happy to see me back? My prayers were answered when Nabi rushed to me, her tiny paws moving elegantly. I practically groveled to the floor to welcome her. Nabi, my precious little Nabi, hadn't failed to make me feel loved. The sadness I received from my interaction with Salem eased with the cuteness of a kitten. Squeals came out of me as I pressed Nabi's cheeks. Everyone stared at me for the exception of Salem, who had yet to look my way.

***

I mentioned we had a date tonight, but nothing came to mind and it would be a waste to use up a whole date on something half thought of. Time was of the essence. I can't imagine what it'll be like when the deal's over. I was so taken aback by Salem's expression that I forgot to pick out a book at the library. On that fishing trip, I had plenty of time to read. There was nothing else to do; no Wi-Fi, no signal. When my dad went to talk with other fishermen, I took these small and occasional opportunities to get a book out. I changed as well, for the better. I never knew reading could be this enjoyable. It's crazy how the mind works when reading. You feel as if you are in a different world. The world around you stops for a moment. It's the only magic I could ever believe in. The magic that made me finish two entire books on a three-day trip. Looking for a book would be the perfect excuse for me to go back there. I'll even get to talk with a certain librarian named Salem. Yes, you see, I'll require some book recommendations. On my way out, I was caught; this time by a fisherwoman—my mom.

"Come to the garden darling, I'd like to introduce you to a guest," she said, holding a tray filled with apple turnovers.

There was nothing I could refuse her. I followed to the garden, taking the tray away from her.

"Who am I meeting exactly?"

"My friend."

"Why am I meeting your friend?"

"She's Salem's mom."

"That changes everything," I said, eager to meet my soon-to-be mother-in-law.

"Why does it change everything? You're close to Salem?"

"More than you can imagine."

Arriving in the garden I saw a woman wearing her hair up, typing away on a laptop, the screen reflected on her glasses.

"Enough with your work, Mel. Look who I brought."

"Oh, you must be Cove," she said, closing her laptop to then place it in inside a pouch on the seat next to her.

"Yes, hello, Mrs. Erise," I said, sitting at the table.

My mom often enjoyed to have some sort of teatime in the afternoon with close friends. It's not the first time she took me to one. There had been other unlucky occasions in the past. Today I considered it lucky. I could ask away about Salem. Nobody would know her better than her own mother. "Cove, don't be shy and take a turnover, or would you prefer a sandwich, a piece of fruit?"

She went all in, whether it was a two-person or five-person tea time. The white ceramic table was filled with plates. From sweet foods such as various store-bought cookies to cake slices to scones with cream and jam and as for salty foods, there were tuna sandwiches, egg sandwiches and corn ships with guacamole on the side. Perhaps my mom had met someone with an appetite as large as her. There was no food wasting with her. As much as she prepared large quantities of food, she ate just as much. Must be where I got my appetite from. Thought right now wasn't the time for food. I was on a mission. I had to use this abrupt meeting.

"I've heard so much about you," she said, putting cream on a scone with a butter knife.

My mouth watered from the sight of the scone, but I managed to get it under.

"I've heard new things about you too, Cove," my mother said. "Since when did you like to read? Apparently, Salem told her you visited the library nearly every day to read."

Yes, that's the only reason I visited the library, to read, no other reasons behind my visits.

"Ha ha, people change," I told her. "Boredom led me to reading. Mrs. Erise, I have a few questions for you regarding Salem," I hurriedly said, with little thought.

I knew I'd needed to ask her about Salem, but what to ask? My mom nudged me by the elbow, a smirk on her face.

"You're curious about Salem?"

I could admit to Salem that I liked her a million times, but in front of others, I found it quite difficult and embarrassing. I couldn't help but scratch the top of my cheek and lose words.

"I'm curious too," Mrs. Erise commented. "My daughter's been different this season and I think I found the cause. Saying the cause makes it seem like a bad thing though trust me, it's been nothing but good. Soon, I feel she'll even end up spending more time with me."

"Really? She changed? Him too!" My mom had to add, making me want to crawl into a hole. "Is there something going on between you two? Oh, it's been my dream for my friend's daughter to marry my son."

Whoa there, I thought. Marriage? That's going too far, too soon. I looked away, not being able to handle the excitement rising on their faces.

"Tell us everything, Cove," added Mrs. Erise. *There's nothing to tell. I'm constantly facing rejection from your daughter. The walls, who seemed to fall down, had only gotten sturdier.*

"There is something I'd like to ask," I said.

"Go ahead," she said, at last taking a bite from the scone she'd held in her hands for the past couple of minutes.

"Did something happen to Salem in the last three days?"

An external factor other than my dystopian theories might have affected her. I am worried about her. And in the end, the most important thing I'd want to hear from her mother is that she's okay. If she isn't, I'll do everything in my power to bring her back.

"Not in my knowledge," she responded. "Why is there something wrong?"

Involving her mom and worrying her wouldn't be the smartest choice, so I shook my head.

"I was just curious about what I've missed while I was away."

What happened to Salem, then?

Chapter 21

No news certainly is good news. Cove hadn't sent me a message with details concerning our outing, and looking at the rising moon outside, I know it won't be coming anytime soon. That date must be cancelled. I reaped what I sowed earlier. With great difficulty, I suppressed my honesty. Hearing his voice, my soul lifted and my feet pressed on the floor, needing to stay put. I couldn't bear to look at him because, when I did for a split second, my mask was cracking. How could it hurt so much to pretend? Have I fallen that deep for him?

'Was it already too late?' I asked myself the entire day.

Where had my aloofness towards his feelings went to, leaving me so vulnerable to the storm. I felt alone again and maybe I was.

The library closed and everyone was home by now, while I hadn't moved an inch from my station. Book after book, I read to distract myself. Scrutinizing every page and every word, I'd retained nothing. I'd forgotten the protagonists' names and couldn't differentiate the conflicts and simple plot points. I wasn't immersed and read without understanding a slight bit. The past three days had been good until he showed up, ruining the happiness I'd regained. Seeing him again made me realize my plan could crumble with ease. A single appearance was more than enough for him to seep into my brain. Ridiculous, isn't it? I have a long way to go if a man can shake my world the way he did. I'm weaker than I thought. From now on, I won't lose. My world will remain intact at the end of the season.

When I stood, my legs felt incredibly heavy. They'd fallen asleep from the long hours I spent on the office chair. Astronauts must have felt this way when they walked on the moon. Perhaps it's more similar to walking in water. Anyhow, now that I'm out of my station, I'd better go home. Before leaving, I'll kiss Nabi goodnight; she hadn't appeared for hours. She must be sleeping on a pile of books somewhere. Her favourite pile is the dark romance pile. The hardcovers weren't covered with sheets of paper, their covers are robust and velvety. Alas, today it seems, she hadn't chosen her all-time favourite, making it hard for me to locate her. I checked between the shelves, inside and outside, but not a black hair on sight. The seat beside the window was my last resort. There weren't that many hiding places in the library. Although seeing she wasn't anywhere I looked made me rethink this statement. It became worrying. It always was easy to spot her. I worried she might have left when someone opened the door—it happened before and I made a town broadcast to find her. Even if the time was late, I'd do the broadcast again and wake up the whole town for Nabi. I called out her name while making my way to the door. It would be wiser to search for her myself in the streets. Who knows, she might be roaming right around the corner. Or better, she may be waiting in front of the door. Cats are smart, they can find their way home. Problem is Nabi doesn't know the way home. She doesn't know the surroundings as she doesn't go past the library's backyard. Before leaving, a green orb caught my eye near a standing lamp. Turning it on, I spotted Nabi beneath it. A sigh of relief and I dropped.

"You found a new hiding place, huh?" I said, caressing her tiny head.

How could one be angry when looking at those doe green eyes? If I caress her too much, Nabi will soon bite my hand. But I couldn't help it. Seeing her so sleepy made it hard to handle. It was unusual for her not to bite me. She didn't even move her head away. She shut her lids ever so slowly and fell asleep again. My mother instincts turned on and I knew something was wrong. I brought her to stand on her four legs. Thankfully she didn't collapse, though her movements were lethargic. That was a sign of sickness. Another and it'll be crystal clear. Food. I checked her bowl, and it was still full, meaning she ate practically nothing today. All day, she must have been too tired to reach high places such as book piles or shelves, hence the new hiding place.

"Don't worry Nabi, I'll bring you to the vet," I told her, taking out my phone to look for vets nearby.

Mardi Town, without a doubt, had plenty of veterinary clinics, though none of them were open late at night. They closed at six like most institutes in their surroundings. Still, I scrolled even to the town next door, but nothing. Nabi had fallen back asleep, and I panicked. I felt the tears rising. It was a first for Nabi to lose energy at night. At this time, she ran around the library, causing me nothing but troubles. I wouldn't be mad if she ran and broke a lamp or collapse a book pile.

"Nabi, don't sleep," I told her, shaking her body gently.

The worst had come to mind when she'd close her eyes. I had to do something. If I were to call the police, would they be able to help? If I brought her to a hospital, would they help? My breath quickened and my cheeks were wet from tears. I scrolled through my contacts list to see if there was someone that could help, one who raises a cat or has a veterinarian family member. My finger stopped on the contact I'd named, 'only speaks in Morse'. He did mention having cats at home. The only person that could help me is the last person I wanted to see. The Universe is working against me. In the end, for Nabi, I called him. With every ring, I attempted to compose myself, only to fail miserably.

"Salem!" his clear voice rang through my ears and, as if being lent a shoulder, I cried more. "What's wrong? Salem! Tell me what's wrong!"

"It's Nabi," I said, my voice cracking.

"What's wrong with Nabi?"

"I think she's sick, but there's nowhere to take her."

"I'm coming. Stay on the phone. Don't hang up. You don't have to talk," he said, rustling sounds being heard.

It was a mistake to call Cove, I was sure of it now, but there was no choice.

"I'm sure it's a common cold," he continued in a voice as equally out of breath as mine. "Nothing will happen to Nabi. I'll be there for you."

His words were magic and one could also say comforting. It didn't end. He kept on talking and reassuring me until he'd reach the front door of the library. And when he came in, he took me in his arms like there's no tomorrow.

"Nabi! Nabi!" I shouted, hitting his shoulders.

My voice had been muffled by the lack of space.

"I know, I know," he said, pulling his head back—only his head. "Don't cry anymore when I'm not there." Now he was insolent enough to pat my face dry with the sleeves of his sweatshirt.

"Nabi..." I'd repeated the only thing on my mind.

"Yes, let's go see Nabi," he'd let go and walked to the lamp where Nabi rested. "What do you think is wrong?" he asked, a sharp look to his eyes.

"She slept all day, hasn't eaten and her movements are slow; this isn't her usual hiding spot. Something clicked in me; I can't exactly explain it."

"I can understand. Nabi's your child and you are able to notice the little things that make a difference."

"Exactly," and just after I said I couldn't explain it. He took the words out of me.

"I'm not a doctor, but I can tell that right now she needs rest and warmth. Wrap her in a blanket and stay close to her, make her drink a bit of water too. Hydration helps."

I nodded and went to find a blanket in the back while he kept her company. Why would a library have blankets, you ask, well we have a space for children and what do they sometimes do? Fall asleep. We stock a couple of them in the back room.

"A wool blanket, perfect," he said, taking it out of my hands.

He rolled it out on the floor and placed Nabi in the middle. Around her, he folded and rolled, putting her in a burrito-like position.

"Now she's even cuter," he said, adjusting the fabric around her face.

"She'll be even cuter when she's back to her normal state."

He smiled. "That's for sure. We'll take her to the vet tomorrow, in case there's something underlying."

'We' he said. He's implying we'll be together in the morning. I hope he's not implying something else. My mind's in the gutter now. My facade had been blown the minute I called him. Feelings, no matter the type, can't be erased when they start to propagate. It's even harder when they're awakened from a long sleep. Cove had caught my eye years ago, lost it for three years and now caught my heart along.

"What do we do now?" I asked him, having both Nabi and *us* in mind.

"What else could we do at midnight?" he said, a smile reaching the corner of his eyes.

"Don't play with me, Cove."

"What did you think I was talking about?" That smile could reach higher places.

"Nothing. I'm as confused as you are."

"Who said I was confused?" He toned down the smile and gave force to his eyes.

"Get on with what you were talking about," was I surrendering with these words?

"I was meaning to have a deep talk with you and right now, it's the only thing we could do. We'll watch over Nabi and talk till the morning. I have so much to tell you and there's so much I want to hear from you."

I hesitated. Having this talk was also something I longed for. I knew nothing about him and was dying of curiosity. Letting him in was another story.

"Shall we move to the sofa?" he said, making it even harder for me to play a role.

"My knees are starting to hurt," I said, indirectly agreeing.

"Here's your child," he said, handing me the burrito after I'd settle on the green leather sofa. He sat right next to me, nearly brushing our skin together. The sofa was small, but not that small.

"I guess we're good now," he said, not looking my way.

"Were we in the wrong?"

"This morning, you weren't yourself. You ignored me and made me think I did something wrong," he answered, a pout forming.

Indeed, you did something wrong Cove. In this situation, I should be the plaintiff and you, the defendant.

"There's nothing wrong, speak. Speak your truth. The one you so desperately wanted to share with me."

"I'm glad you're back," he started, "but you're putting me on the spot. I can't suddenly think of a truth. I thought we'd let it flow as conversations are supposed to."

"Where do we start?"

"How about the last three days?" He said, his voice now matching the ambience of the calm night.

"I have nothing to say about the past days."

Saying anything would admit my feelings and that's the last thing I'd want to do.

"I'll start then. You'll open up later." His voice smoothed out like whisky.

I won't fall deeper if that's what you want, Cove.

"I became even more confused on this trip. My dad's words were hard to digest."

I let him speak, having the feeling he'd answer the questions I had in mind in due time. Tonight, I'll be the listener.

"You see, this summer is an intermission to my life. It never was my plan to come back to Mardi Town. I was called to."

Intermission? He knows the term intermission. I didn't know Cove could get sentimental. Was this a hidden game mode of his?

"I came to get clear," he'd said, leaving more questions than answers.

"With who?" I asked as if he had a fight to get back to.

"With myself. This year I was Peter Pan, but I want to grow up now. I've had enough of being lost. The problem is, growing up doesn't have a good image in my head. Is it worth it to walk on a road I know won't make me happy?"

I don't know the details about the conversation he shared with his father, but I can presume it was a little something about society's standards. That would explain Cove's messed up view. I'm not saying the manner his brain works is wrong. No. I'm saying that he only sees a side of the world. He's the closed off one, not me.

"Why do you think you'll end up unhappy?" I asked him, knowing the answer.

"I'll work a 9 to 5 job that doesn't particularly interest me till the day I can retire and live my life. By then, I might be too old to enjoy life as I could in now." I lack the fingers to count the times I've heard this answer.

"What makes you think you won't be interested in your job?"

"Do you even know what I'm studying?"

"You never told me."

He turned his body towards me as if we weren't close enough. I couldn't see his eyes, though; the library wasn't well light at night. Some lights were scheduled and couldn't be directly switched on. I only had a couple of standing lamps at my disposition. None were near the sofa, which made me nervous. It could also be a relief to not see his features. His voice is dangerous as it is.

"Economics," he said, the word travelling through my right ear only.

"Do you like this subject?"

"I hate it."

That snapped me back to reality.

"That's the first mistake you made. No wonder you think you'll end up unhappy."

"I had no other choice..."

"Excuses."

"It wasn't easy to choose a major. Nothing matched my preferences. I ended up going with the popular choice." Cove tried to defend his choice, but I'd just made the conviction to break down that wall he himself could not see.

"And you still don't see your mistake? Going with the popular choice isn't for everyone. And it's the worst you can do when lost; to pick at random. That won't make it easier for you. You're the living proof of that."

"I know." I could vaguely see his shoulders dropping. He'd been caught and seemed as vulnerable as a caged bird. The puppy turned into a bird.

"Making one mistake doesn't mean it's over."

Unknowingly, I had turned into an inspirational talker. It was surprising since I'd rejected self-help books. I made a pinky promise with myself to not read a self-help book even after death. It's a question of personal preferences. Don't listen to me and get this type of book if you need it.

"What does it mean, then?"

I turned into an old man with a white beard talking to a young man that had a lost his way in the mountains in search of a hidden treasure.

"I don't need to explain something this easy. Haven't people told you to learn from mistakes? Did you witness the existence of a person who's never made mistakes? Life is a path of trial and errors."

My toes curled alone since my fingers were busy supporting Nabi. Those words, they do seem like they'd come out of a self-help book and I never thought I'd see the day they'd come out of my mouth.

"Tell me, how do I fix my mistake?" he said.

"I can't tell you. You need to figure it out yourself."

"How? People always tell me I need to resolve my problems by myself, but I really have no clue."

I had the clue he needed; the answer as well. Though the epiphany would be much more powerful if he found it himself.

"With time," I said, fully knowing it'll

frustrate him.

"How much time?"

This I couldn't answer. Like him, I hated when people told me to be patient and that everything passes *with time*. I still carry this hatred for time. Nothing seemed to have passed for me. The wait was fruitless until Cove arrived. Even that will be taken away from me.

"As much as you need."

Chapter 22

He's not here. Cove said we'd go to the vet together. Carrying a well-rested Nabi in her carrier, I went alone. To be fair, we did stay up late talking and anyone would sleep through their alarm. I hadn't agreed for him to come either. If I really wanted him to come, I would've called or sent a message at least. Anyhow, thankfully, the vet said that Nabi had caught a common cold and that it seems she's already doing better. I nearly hugged the vet when hearing the good news. Though I was reminded of Cove since he'd told me the same last night. He reassured me and took care of Nabi. It's getting difficult to explain how I felt about Cove. One word comes to mind each time: safe. If I was running from something, he'd be the one waiting on the other end; with open arms. And I was always reluctant to jump in these arms. Because then, it'll be too late to turn back. And so I kept running, avoiding everything and everyone around me. Pulling down the edges of my baby blue shorts, I <u>braved</u> the sunlight. I should have brought a hat. This paisley fabric headscarf isn't covering much. Right now, I'm standing in front of Glass Wing, wishing I were inside. To take Nabi to the vet, I needed to take the morning off, but when I came back, Ms. Elgnis kicked me out, saying she'd written me off for a full day and exiled me from the library. She physically pushed me out and is standing on the other side of the door to guard it. I am banished from my favourite place. My shelter. It doesn't make sense and left me with nowhere to go. It'd be a waste to spend this rare day off at home either. Let me back in the library. I'd rather work than be out on such a hot day. Wearing a t-shirt and shorts, I'll get sun-burnt in no time. Sunscreen or not, today's sun will do ravages. Perhaps I should stay under a tree's shadow. If only I had a book for that; my day might turn peaceful. I can't even go to the library. I suppose I could buy a book from a bookstore. Yes, that'll do. Right then, as I'd made my decision; my hands on the long strap of my bag, I'd perceive a figure from afar. A small one that got bigger by the second. Approaching, I'd recognized him. That figure was none other than Cove. He dashed towards me in the span of seconds and had stopped with not even a meter separating us.

"I'm sorry!" he said, breathless. Cove squatted down, resting his hands on his bare knees. "It's been a while since I ran," he said, lifting his head.

However,There I had a déjà vu moment. The sweat dripping down his hair to his cheeks. The muscle driven legs. The training shorts, although they were of a different colour, midnight blue, they still bore a resemblance. I'd seen this exact Cove multiple times a few years back. That's the Cove I knew. That's the guy I had a crush on. However, I shouldn't be fooled by his appearance. He'd given up on his passion. He simply ran because he feared we'd miss each other.

"I'm sorry for not coming in the morning. I slept through my alarm that my mom turned off without waking me up."

"It's alright," I told him.

"How's Nabi?" He said now lifting his body from that squatting position.

"She's fine. It was just a cold."

"That's good. That's great. That's fantastic!" he exclaimed, opening his arms to the sky.

"I'll get going then," I said, walking down the steps.

The humid air started getting to me. I hadn't run like him, but I felt sweat dripping down my back. This is no place to stand. My book and my tree waited for me.

"Wait!" he said, grabbing my wrist. "We have a date."

"I was not informed of it," I said, wanting to rip out his beautiful blond hair.

"I didn't have the time to inform you. It's an impromptu date."

I clenched my fingers on the strap and turned around.

"You're just saying that to keep me from leaving."

"No, no." He placed another hand on my arm, slightly above the wrist. "I really do have a plan for today. Trust me."

Trust me, he said, tempting me. I never knew I longed to hear such a line.

"Where to?"

"I can't tell you."

"Then you're lying."

"Who says I am."

How frustrating.

"Trust me," he said again.

I wholeheartedly wanted to. So I took a blind step towards Cove and reminded him that "it's a friendly outing, not a date!"

"Let's see how long you'll keep denying it," he said, letting go of my arm and walking ahead.

"I should be the one saying that."

"Yeah, yeah." He waved back his hand.

Comeback of the bickering. That's the name of our corner on the daily talk show.

I pulled on his jersey, and when he turned to face me, I bleeped. Had I gone back to five-years-old?

"Who's the childish one now?" he remarked.

"No matter how hard I try, I'll never reach your level of childishness. Now tell me where we are going."

"If I tell you, you might not want to go anymore."

"Regardless of the place, it's not like I want to go on this outing anyway."

"You have a point," he said.

"Then tell me."

Knowing where we'd have our friendly outing would give me time to prepare myself mentally.

"School. We're going to school."

"What?" I stopped in my tracks and immediately grabbed the edge of his jersey, creasing it. "What do you mean by that?"

"We're visiting Mardi High. There's no one there. It's the summer, remember?"

"Right..."

I forgot that the school would be empty. I was nervous, thinking we'd meet old teachers or getting embarrassed in classes full of kids. Weird of me to think about that. I don't have any trauma associated with school, but I can admit it wasn't my favourite place. It was simply a bridge to adulthood. I walked the hallways with a book in hand every day until I'd reached graduation. From then on, I could live my life. School was but a passage.

"We are going?" he asked me, and I was still tugging on the fabric of his shirt.

"I suppose we are," I assured, letting go.

There's no need to be afraid of that place. As there is no reason for me to refuse this outing. Nothing of mine remains there.

***

There they were, the cement coloured walls of this edifice we called school. A pain manifested itself in my stomach, reminding me of every first day of school. Nerves show themselves in various ways. I'm sure it's different for Cove. The only pain his stomach could feel at the moment would be hunger. As a social butterfly, seeing the school will only bring back good memories. We may both be sad about school, but for different reasons. While he misses it, I'd long for the end of our trip to memory lane.

"We're here, pretty Salem. It's Mardi High," he said, black metal bars facing him.

"Yes, we're here, and we might as well leave. How do you intend on entering when clearly it's closed?" I said, seeing the lock on the closed gate. "Unless you're a very capable locksmith, there's no going in."

"Salem, Salem, Salem. Do you really think I forgot the gate was locked?" He looked at me, his eyebrows raised. "We're jumping over it."

My heart dropped.

"Oh no," I said.

I never climbed a gate and never envisaged to. Why would I. This is to prove Cove is a lunatic.

"I'll help you. We'll climb together, bar by bar. I'll jump down the other side first, then I'll help you. It's going to be easy. Trust me."

There he goes again with this, *trust me.* And here I went again—hypnotized by comforting words.

"Give me your hand," he said, extending his.

Once I gave it to him, he placed it on a bar. I quickly took it off since it was sizzling hot. Tapping it a couple of times, my hand acclimated to it.

"Put your right foot there, and the left here," he said, pointing at all the appropriate places, making sure I was well set before climbing himself. "We'll take it from here," he said, taking slow steps so that I could follow safely. "We're not in a hurry. No one passes by this reclusive area, so take your time and watch your step."

Starting from the cement coloured walls, the area surrounding the school was grey. The grass was crisp, and for the most part, dead. The building was built farther from the main attractions. You can imagine that my school life was even more bleak with this environment. Withstanding the heat against my skin, I climbed up the gate, Cove eyeing me from the top.

'Wrong day to wear short,' I thought.

The metal received direct hits from the sun, and I guess you could cook an egg here. The things I do for Cove.

"You're almost there," he said, waiting for me to reach the top.

"It's not that easy," I complained, holding the bars for dear life.

"You're doing well for your first time."

Cove him was a chimpanzee. How could he reach the top so fast? My eyes had been busy focusing on the bars I'd needed to climb, but still I took the opportunity to watch his long legs extending. I am ashamed of myself. Then, without notice, Cove leaped on the other side and I froze, my mouth wide open.

"You want me to do that?" I said, thinking that the shock must have broken his legs. However, he walked fine and even jumped around waving his arms playfully.

"I'll hold you and put you on the ground. It can be dangerous for you. Our legs are very different. I'm an ex-athlete."

Ex, he said. My heart broke when he mentioned it, since I knew how happy he was when the word ex wasn't attached to his status. Yet again, I couldn't muster the courage to ask him about it. I'd let it go and focused on the urgency of the current situation. One leg was on the school's side and the other was outside.

"You can't come down like that," he said, looking from the ground. "Bring your other leg to this side. It's alright, I'm here for you."

Hearing that, I brought my legs forth, bracing for a fall that in the end didn't happen. There was enough space on the gate for me to sit down. However, my bottom and my thighs were burning. I just know that my skin will start to chip in a few days.

"Come down now," he said, holding his arms out.

As if I'd trust him with my bones. He must have noticed the hesitation in me and nodded.

"I'm here to catch you. You will not even touch the floor. Just throw yourself at me," he said. "Like a bird, fly to me."

He kept saying strange things for me to hurry up and it worked. I couldn't hear anymore of it and leaped with closed eyes—not my best decision. Expecting to touch the floor, I was surprised to feel arms around my waist. I'd latched onto Cove and he held on me so tightly my feet were dangling in the air. When I opened my eyes, I stared directly into his. The smile on his face had disappeared and contrary to how I'd imagined it to be, it was far from terrifying. I don't know whether jumping from a gate made my heart race or if it was due to being held by Cove. We both didn't dare to speak and kept on looking. Our faced were mere inches away, and it became hard to control one of my senses, the touch. If my lips had eyes, they'd be looking very closely.

"I'm heavy, aren't I?" I told him, hoping he'd let me down.

"Not only you flew to me like a bird, but you're as light as one of their feathers."

"Stop lying and let me down." I hit his chest to make him lose balance.

"Alright, alright. For your own safety, I'll let you down."

Not looking back, I walked to the door and, as expected, it was locked. My red hand burned even more when I attempted to twist the knobs.

"There's no space to go over this one," I said. "And don't tell me you'll break the door."

"No, that would be going too far."

Oh, now it's too far. Even Cove had limits.

"We'll have to settle for the yard," he said, his smile still nowhere to be found.

His gaze towards the yard was dead inside. The yard was mainly a running track, and it seemed to displease Cove as he had no choice but to walk through it, seeing we came all the way here. This is the only memory lane available. And so we walked along it, avoiding the lane itself. Cove seemed to be distracted on the way. His voice grew quiet and his eyes stuck to the soil. For once, I was the one to initiate a conversation. I had no choice.

"What did you want to do here, Cove?"

There must be a reason why he used up a friendly outing on this. Each outing had a purpose.

He raised his head, looking like he'd awoken from a deep slumber and was brought to the middle of nowhere.

"Oh, I wanted to brush up on our school memories. Seems like we can't."

It wasn't like him to speak in such a disheartened tone.

"Who says we can't?" I said, crossing my arms.

I was about to hit where it hurts. There's

no use avoiding it in any longer. At this rate, Cove will stay a lost child his entire life. He needs to know his options in order to take a decision. And if the universe isn't going to bring him the epiphany he'd needed, I'll do it. In their stead, I'll show him what he could have if he tried.

"There's not much to reminiscence about in the yard," he said, tugging the end of his jersey.

Using all the strength I could assemble, I pushed him to the tracks. I stared directly into his deep blue and misty eyes only to shout, "Run you idiot! I know You're dying to!"

At first, he showed me the face of a confused puppy. Then he gazed at the track and then back at me. It went on for a whole minute before he bit his bottom lip and went for it. Cove ran again. He dashed towards a line visible to the eyes of the passionate ones. Nostalgia swells as I see him running. He spreads memories behind him with every stride. And his laughter rings like an echo in the school yard.

Welcome back home, Cove.

Chapter 23

Following that day, things have been quieter. I have seen little of Cove, which was strange. He hadn't stepped foot in the library, nor did he contact me as often. He occasionally sent good morning and goodnight messages, but that was it. He was secretive of his days and I didn't pry—that would be breaking character. He's supposed to be the actively curious one. I'd have questions in mind, but hoped he'd answer them himself when he blabbered on. Though I hadn't had much luck with this method since he didn't blabber about himself too often. But enough of this. I can't think about it all day. Mostly not today. Saturday June 10th, 2023. It is none other than the Glass Wing annual picnic day. The day I've waited for ages. One I also was supposed to share with Cove. He's a volunteer, remember?

Yet he's neglecting his duties by being late. The event was almost starting, and I needed his help with the preparations. Instead, I had to request help from Ms. Elgnis and the weekend staff. So much to prove I could do it all by myself. In actual fact, help was needed to set things I'd prepared alone. Thus, you could say I proved myself. Well, it's too early to say that; the event had yet to start and successfully end.

"Everything's going according to plan?" asked Ms. Elgnis, making her way towards me.

"It seems," I said, enjoying the breeze.

We were having the picnic in front of the library where a field of grass allowed us to accommodate numerous people. I've decorated the space with garlands hanging from tree to tree and balloons held down by sand bags I placed here and there. I've added some mats since I knew many would forget theirs or simply didn't know they'd needed to bring one. The lemonade stand stood in a corner while my hands smelled like lemons from all the squeezing I did. As for my cookies, they were stored in the fridge. I'd made a hundred the previous day. As soon as I finished my workday, I made a quick trip to the supermarket and worked my bottom off, only to finish at midnight. Even then, I imagined baking with Cove. If he were there, the cookies would have been done at a much later time since he'd play around throwing flour at me and I'd have no choice but to get my revenge. Nevertheless, it would have been fun. Where is Cove? I hate to admit it, but I do miss seeing his face around and hearing his voice.

"I'm glad the weather's on our side," said Ms. Elgnis. "Do you remember the picnic it rained, years ago?"

"Of course. If only it'd started in the morning, we would have cancelled the picnic."

Years ago, in the middle of the Glass Wing picnic, a downpour fell on us. The day had been sunny and the weather forecast had said nothing about rain. Everyone was wet, and the food was ruined. Everyone laughed about the sudden rain party, but it soon became too messy to handle. Inevitably, the mats grew dirty with mud and became of no use. The picnic could no longer go on and people were sent back home. Cleaning was tough on that particular day. The funniest thing is that the rain stopped not too long after. In the end, it didn't matter. What was done was done. The rain had been so heavy, the yard turned into a swimming pool. One minute sufficed to make the picnic impossible.

"I trust mother nature to give us peace today," she said, looking at the sky.

"Don't fail us, mother nature," I continued, making her laugh.

"I'll leave you to work; I suppose there are still things you need to take care of. Every year, there's at least something that requires extra attention. Nothing ever goes perfectly to plan," she said, scaring me.

"Is this supposed to be a curse?"

"No, no, I hope there's nothing wrong. I was only speaking from experience."

Experiences are different for everyone. Surely nothing will happen. I mean, what could go wrong? It's a picnic, not a film's premier. Most things were ready, I'm just waiting for the author guest to arrive as well as the musicians. Unless they bail, this event will be flawless. The thought of it alone gives me the shudders.

"Miss Salem! Miss Salem, we're here!" shouted the kids from the reading club as they ran towards me.

"My little helpers are here," I said, ruffling their small heads of hair.

I asked them to come early for them to learn how the lemonade stand works.

"We're going to be rich!" Jay, a little boy, said, holding on to the pockets of his pants.

"No, we're not!" Jane, a little girl, said, hitting his arm. "The money's not for us. It's for the reading club!"

"But we're in the reading club. It is for us!" he shouted back.

Like the children they were, they fought and bickered about banal affairs. It's no question about who's right or wrong, it's about who will crack first. I won't let it get there.

"Kids, there's no time to waste. You need to get behind the stand and listen to the instructions."

"Yes, miss Salem," they grumbled.

It felt good to have the least bit of authority. Where else would I have it if not for the job of librarian? I'm not planning on getting married or have children of my own. This is as close as it gets for me.

"When someone asks for a glass of lemonade, you place a paper cup under the faucet of the large glass bottle, then you twist the faucet on, letting the lemonade go down until you fill the cup. Be careful not to over fill it. Twist the faucet off and hand the glass to the customer. Meanwhile, one of you will take the money from the customer and place it in the piggy bank. To recap, one person will take care of the cups, one will take care of opening and closing the faucet and one will take care of the money. Got it?"

"I want to take care of the money!" said Jay. I expected no less.

"I'll handle the faucet. I don't trust these two boys. They'll forget to close it and make a mess," Jane said, eyeing the boys the way you'd look at dirt.

"Hey! Who says I'll forget? Maybe Jay, but not me," said Danny at his turn.

"Hey!" Jay snapped.

As much as this was an entertaining sight, I had important things to do.

"I'll take my leave now. Don't fight too long and if you run out of lemonade, tell me; I made plenty."

I don't know if they heard this part. They were so busy running their mouths about who's the responsible one. It was then that things started to go downhill. I'd felt a buzz in my pocket and, without a clue of what was going to happen, I picked up the phone.

"I'm so sorry Salem," were the first words I heard coming from the voice of a man in his thirties. "I'm Onder Land, the author of The Hidden Time. I'm afraid I'll be running late and may not even make it to the picnic. I'll try my best, but the traffic in Tempo town is horrible today."

I couldn't talk back, feeling the shock hitting me too hard. My flawless event had earned a flaw. Why was he in Tempo town? It's one of our neighbouring towns but if he had an event perhaps he should have planned to be in town a day before. And how bad could the traffic be in such a small town? There's a reason it's not called a city.

"Hello? Salem?"

"Yes, I'm here. Please come. Even if you end up being late, you must come."

"I'll try my best." He muttered identical words earlier.

Like that, the call ended, and I was left pacing back and forth in the field. People had started to come lay their mats, and I noticed another missing element. It was much too quiet. Even the wind blew elsewhere rather than on our property. There was no music!

The musicians had yet to be seen, and neither was their equipment. I told them to come early. Everyone should have been here by now. I couldn't believe that the responsible ones on this day were elementary kids. They came in time and were already at work while the adults... Even Cove. I'm fairly disappointed he's not here. Even if he weren't a volunteer, he'd come to cheer me on. Right now, I needed to hear comforting words from him. I'd needed to find shelter in him. Where will I get the strength to fix this situation? Just then I was reminded of a passage of a book I read years ago: 'As long as you don't forget this person, even if it rains or snows, they'll come back to you.' Perhaps, if I believed strongly enough, this passage will prove itself to be true. Cove's existence was engraved in my mind; I didn't need to try hard.

Now for the musicians. A call hadn't arrived from them, thus they must be running late. If I attempt to call them, they'll apologize and say they're on their way, right? And so I did.

"Hello?"

"Who is this?" they said, throwing a knife at my heart.

"It's Salem, the librarian. You're supposed to come play at the picnic…" My voice grew quieter. I was annoyed to have to explain it again. Have they not saved my number? It wasn't our first phone call.

"Did we have a gig at the library today?" He said probably not to me but a teammate, seeing the volume was lower.

"Did we?" another said.

It's not that I waited for their conversation to be over, it's that I felt the sky falling on me and was too stunned to say anything.

"I think we double gigged. Cancel the library. This one's more important."

The audacity of this band to forget about us and cancel the day of.

"So, Salem, was it? I'm sorry but we can't make it. We're in the middle of another gig. We'll send back the money sometimes this month. How much did you pay us?"

I didn't want to answer with words, however, what could I do? We talked on the phone. I hanged up. Yes, that's what I did. I'll take care of them in due time. Now's the time to resolve the problem, not curse out others. It took me weeks to find local musicians interested in a picnic gig for a reasonable price; how can I do it again in less than fifteen minutes? Mother nature was on my side but the universe wasn't. It's one or the other, I guess. You can't have it all would say Ms. Elgnis if she found out what was happening.

Where are you Cove? I thought to myself minute after minute.

"Hey, Salem!" From afar, a woman ran to me, a man next to her.

It took me long enough to realize it was the barista who worked at the Cherry Street coffee shop.

"You remember me, right? I'm Sol," she placed her hand on her chest.

"Yes, I do. I'm sorry, I was overwhelmed by problems and zoned out."

"Problems? What problems? Share them with me. Three heads would work better than one," she said, pointing to the man who held her hand. He smiled, his lips curved more upwards rather than sideways. Though it was different, it reminded me of Cove's. His lips rose sideways, just like the joker. How I wish I could see this smile. It would lift at least some of my worries. Some.

"The musicians bailed at the last minute, and there's no one I can call."

Sol turned to face the man whose eyes lit up. "Uh, I may be a far cry from a musician, but I'm learning to play the guitar."

"This is Eugene, by the way, and he's an excellent guitarist, now and in a past life of his," Sol said.

They looked at each other, tenderness filling their eyes.

"I can get my guitar in five minutes," he continued.

"I'd be very grateful, but would that be okay with you? You're here to enjoy the picnic."

"Playing the guitar is fun for me. I'd still be enjoying myself," he said, his eyes crinkling.

Like that, one of my problem was resolved. Soon, a lovely sound of strings would feel the air. It's funny how a brief encounter turned out to be of help. Maybe the universe awoke.

"Thank you Sol," I told her as she stood waiting for Eugene, who went to get his guitar.

"I'm glad I met you," she said, making me feel something; butterflies. "Seeing you here again makes it feel like destiny. We should take this chance and become friends. Would you like to become my friend?"

"I'd love to," I responded the moment she

finished speaking.

My first friend is a girl named Sol. I can't believe the day where I could say that I had a friend of my age would come. I couldn't even make one in a school filled to the brim and here I am befriending someone I'd met for the second time. Her words touched me to the point of having butterflies.

"You know, you're the first friend I made. You see, I was home-schooled," Sol told me, surprising me. "It's difficult to meet anyone in that situation."

"I wasn't home-schooled, but I too never had friends before."

"Really?"

"It's a first for both of us. Must be fate."

"Definitely!"

"What about Eugene? How did you find a guy like him?" I asked.

"Fate. With him too, fate linked us together. Otherwise we would have never met."

"Coincidentally, I have a similar story. I might not have friends, but there is a guy who recently came out of the blue."

She stared at me, her moss-green eyes shining like crystals. "And you took a liking to him, right?" Sol nudged my shoulder. "Right?"

"Yes. I like him." For the first time, I had admitted my feeling for him.

It was refreshing while simultaneously painful. My feelings were worth nothing if the recipient wasn't there. If I'm left alone in Mardi Town, then there is no meaning to this confession. It couldn't be helped. My eyes watered and I left the tears escape from them. Sol took a hold of me and I think she spoke, but I couldn't properly hear her in the midst of my world crumbling. The sky really was falling on me.

"I told you not to cry if I'm not with you." These words I heard loud and clear. It could only be him.

Turning around to the source of the voice I longed to hear, I saw Cove. Wearing the same purple jersey he wore back in high school, he stood, a cheeky smile to him.

"Cove!"

He walked towards me and grabbed my hand.

"I'm sorry, I need to borrow her for a second," he said to Sol, who now had a smile on her face.

"Take her," she said.

Without a word, he dragged me inside the

library. Many questions filled my head, yet I was quiet. With round eyes, I stared at him. All the rage he caused me eased in a single second. It's unfair. I wonder if he'd felt the same way at least once. I wonder if seeing me has this effect on him. He confessed first, but I fell harder. Would his feelings rival mine?

"I missed you," he said, shamelessly.

If you missed me so much, why didn't you come to the library?

He continued on, "I was busy the last few days. Ever since you pushed me to the tracks, I felt freed. You released me from that stupid cage I built myself. I realized there were only two things that make me as happy as can be. The first one is to be with you and the second is running."

He had his epiphany, just as I did.

"I'm lucky that all my happiness is in Mardi Town," he said, making me raise a brow.

"All?"

"Yes, all. I'm staying, Salem. I joined the track team of Mardi Town and am planning to stay with you till the end."

"By the end, you mean death?"

He grew closer to me, a hair separating us.

"What else would it be?"

"Why would you stay? With the amount of passion you have, I'm sure you'll make it elsewhere, in the city."

"How could I leave when I heard the woman I love saying she liked me?"

"You heard me?"

"Loud and clear."

An invisible hair the length of Nabi's separated us. It was nerve racking while also exciting.

"Can I?" he asked.

I didn't need superpowers to understand what he meant. With a nod, I let him. I let him crash his lips on mine. If the sun and the moon collided, the explosion would be incomparable. That's what it felt like. Two hearts merging and exploding in the midst. A first kiss, a first lover, a first friend, a first picnic. Picnic? Picnic! Right, the picnic is still going on. People were settling in when I left. Eugene went to get his guitar and the author... I pushed Cove away in a hurry.

"Cove, it's all very nice, but I need to get back. My career depends on this."

I ran out of the library. And as soon as I opened the door, a gentle melody flowed to my ears. Eugene had arrived with the guitar and sat near a tree in the centre while people happily swayed their heads, holding each a cup of lemonade from the stand who seems to be successful. Even if the guest author I invited doesn't come, it'll still be deemed a success. A humble gathering of people can be just as entertaining.

"I'm so sorry Salem. I'm here!" exclaimed a man, catching his breath.

It seems there's nothing to worry about anymore. The author is here, there's good music, people are happy but mostly, Cove came out of the library and stood by me.

"You should have been more attentive to time," he said to Mr. Land. "How ironic that your book's name is the hidden time. I guess it was really hidden from you."

We exploded in laughter from his comment, and I took hold of Cove's hand. I promised I'd never let go of it.

My Glass Wing Butterfly flapped its wings, however, it stayed near and I'd decided to follow wherever it went.

The End

Acknowledgements

Thank you to the reader who picked up this book. If you've made it this far; I hope it was enjoyable.

Thank you to a passionate group of people who inspired me to work just as hard.

I also wanted to thank myself for working so hard. Writing, editing and publishing a book is no easy task. Let's keep it going for the many books to come.

The Mardi Town Series

Deja Vu On Cherry Street (November 18)

Once In A Glass Wing (May 18)

Other stand-alones coming out in the near future!